I0555724

C is for Chainsaw and Other Dark Tales

John Opalenik

ISBN 978-1-7333177-6-4

Written by John Opalenik
Cover art by Amanda Opalenik
Edited by Nancy Manning

Printed in The United States of America

Visit www.johnopalenik.com

Contents

The person in my life who inspired me most is…was, one of the dozens of people I've seen chained up in the basement of the house where I grew up. Even one sentence in, I know I can't submit this to the college admissions board, but before I pen something more palatable, I have to tell the truth. I have to tell you about where I came from, what he did for me, and how I got out.

The family's house lay waiting like a hungry black hole deep in the woods, but close enough to a back road that people would get stuck there. Either by misjudging when they should have gassed up or if they blew a tire driving through the debris on the unmaintained road. Eventually, they'd realize that there's no cell service anywhere near here and start looking for help. If they stayed on the road, my brother, Spike would conveniently show up with his tow truck. In the winter, when the foliage isn't as thick, people would sometimes notice the subtle glow of our fireplace, and they would come to us.

C is for Chainsaw

Whether it was Titus, the man I thought of as my father, talking his prey into a false sense of security until they were already at the top of the basement stairs, or Spike sneaking up on them with a hammer and dragging them into the house kicking and screaming, the result was the same. They'd be trapped in our basement as long as we could keep them alive, and piece by piece, they'd end up on our dinner table.

That's what happened to Kenneth Adamson, the man who saved me, and the person who has inspired me the most. Yes, that Kenneth Adamson. The beloved children's author who went missing ten years ago. Everyone who followed the case knows that he went missing somewhere between Philly and Boston. I can't say where, because even though I'm deleting this essay after I write it, I can't bring myself to write a detail that could lead to people finding the family I grew up in and exposing the life I left behind. I tell myself it's because revealing who I was and what I did would undo everything that Kenneth did for me and drag me back into a world he wanted me to escape, but sometimes in quiet moments, I wonder if I'm still protecting them out of some sick sense of loyalty.

He and his publicist, I never caught his name, were driving between events on tour promoting his back-to-back releases, an alphabet book for toddlers, and a picture book for the older siblings. A thunderstorm led to several branches and even a few trees blocking access to the back roads they were using as a shortcut, and they tried to find a detour. Instead, they found us.

They agreed that the publicist would cut through the woods to make it to the faint glow of our cabin in the distance. He reasoned that we must have a chainsaw and other tools to help clear the branch out of the road. Kenneth remained with the car as their backup plan. If it got dark and his publicist couldn't find his way , Kenneth would honk the horn to lead him back. Spike had me open the door when he knocked, so he could use the distraction to sneak up on him and hit him in the back of the head with the rubber mallet-style hammer he used when he didn't want to kill right away. Normally, Spike was so well-practiced, he could knock someone out without breaking bones or drawing much blood. This time, the publicist staggered forward trying to catch himself, and instead of stopping him, I recoiled. He managed to stumble through the kitchen door by the time Spike caught up to him and grabbed at him with his thick sausage fingers. The dazed man pulled away as he tripped through the doorway and hit his head on the corner of our kitchen table on his way down.

Then the blood started to flow.

"Is he dead, Dad?" I looked up at Titus, who'd been in the kitchen sharpening his knives.

"No, he ain't dead!" Titus shouted. "Get that dishtowel and the duct tape and wrap his head up."

C is for Chainsaw

I obediently got to work but paused when I saw the extent of his injuries. "His head's dented and one of his eyes is pointed the wrong way."

Titus turned his attention to Spike. "God damn it, Spike. When it ain't winter, we've got to make them last. Can't carve him up and keep him in an icebox until it's cold out here." He looked down at his dark flannel shirt to check it for bloodstains and slicked back his greasy hair. "Get him in the basement and make sure he don't bleed out. Now I've got to get his buddy into the basement without a scratch on him or a bunch of meat's going to go to waste."

Spike grabbed him under each arm and dragged him to the basement, shielding his head from any additional damage, but not sparing the rest of his body as he dragged him downstairs. He undressed the man's limp body before tying him down to the chopping block. Spike tossed the clothes at me. "Run through his pockets. Put any cash in the jar in the sitting room, and if you find a phone, give it to Dad. He'll toss it in the river on the other side of the state line. Then wash those pants. They look like they might fit me, but I'm pretty sure he pissed himself when he went down."

I heard Titus talking Kenneth into the house, saying that his buddy was waiting in the other room until the tow truck could come get them. It wasn't until he opened the door and saw that Titus had led him to the basement that he knew something was wrong. I wasn't surprised. People foolish enough not to suspect anything until they're actually at the bottom of the basement stairs are pretty rare. I don't know exactly how it happened because I was going through the other guy's pockets at the time, but Titus must have taken out the double-barreled shotgun while Kennth's back was turned and forced him to shackle himself to the basement wall . Otherwise, I'm not sure how he could have got him down there without a scratch on him.

The next day, Titus went into town for supplies while Spike took apart the car Kenneth was driving, looking for parts that would either be compatible with one of our vehicles or could be sold on one of Titus's rare trips into town. My job was to sort through their luggage and set aside anything valuable. I opened a crate full of books and even though Titus said books weren't useful for anything but kindling and toilet paper, I paused. There were dozens of copies of the same two books, and they were full of pictures of kids like me. Well, not exactly like me. These kids looked nourished and cared for. Their clothes were bright primary colors instead of the earth tones that all clothes turned after a few months in the cabin. They all looked so happy.

I hadn't seen many other kids. Titus always said they were more trouble than they were worth. Not enough meat on their bones, and if a kid goes missing, people will search and stir up trouble. He always said that hitchhikers or young adults with out-of-state plates were best.

C is for Chainsaw

Something about seeing the illustrations of kids with smiling faces made me think that maybe there could be more to life than what I'd been doing as long as I could remember. I shoved one copy of it under my mattress and put the rest in the burn pile.

***

The next time I went into the basement to change out Kenneth's shit bucket, I started to notice how Kenneth was different from most people who ended up in the basement. Rather than begging, threatening, or screaming until his vocal cords shredded, he looked at me with a sad drop in his gaze when he realized I was only a child. "Are they taking care of you, kid? When's the last time you had a bath or ate a piece of fruit?"

I thought back to the last time I ventured down to the river's edge to rinse off. It had been a while. If my hair got wet in the winter, it would be frozen by the time I got back to the cabin. "I got a roof over my head and food in my belly. What more can someone ask for in this world?" I parroted the line Titus taught me, and I almost convinced myself I believed.

I'd seen a lot of people looking sorry for themselves chained to the basement wall over the years, but he showed a different type of sadness. "There's a whole world out there. Once you see it, you'll know that there's a lot more to the world than staying warm and fed." His eyes went from his lap, up to me. "What's your name, kid?"

I hesitated. Nobody had ever asked me that before. "Elijah."

The door slammed upstairs and I knew Titus got back from a trip into town. "I've got to go. Give me your shit bucket."

"Call it a toilet bucket." He handed it to me. "It's nice to meet you, Elijah. I'm Kenneth."

***

The next time Spike and Titus were out of the house, I brought the book downstairs. "Why did you have so many of these?"

"I wrote it." He tilted his head, forming his next question. "Did you read it?"

"What's it about?" I knew that books told stories, but hadn't read one before.

"They didn't teach you how to read." Kenneth looked truly heartbroken. "Ever been to school?"

"Tell me the story." I handed him the book.

Kenneth opened the book and read each page, giving each character its own voice and pausing to talk about the pictures and let me ask questions. Most of them were about whether there were families like the one in the book. The story was about a little boy who was afraid to go swimming in the pool but didn't want his cousins to find out. The boy's mother took him swimming every day and let him spend as long as he wanted circling the shallow end while still clinging to the edge of the pool. She let him feel comfortable and ready to let go and swim across to the other side. I imagined what Titus would have done if that were me. He'd have thrown me in and waited for me to splash my way back out. Then, if there was a reason he wanted me to know how to swim, he'd have kept throwing me in until I got good at swimming back out. Simple, and brutally effective.

Kenneth finished the story and looked at his surroundings, piecing together what my family had been doing for generations. "Why do they do this?"

I thought back to the many times people have wailed, "Why are you doing this?" as Titus or Spike carved pieces off them. Their answer was simple. "A man's got to eat." After sharing his story with me, I felt like I owed Kenneth a real answer. "I do it because they did it. They started doing it because Grandpa did it. Grandpa used to say that they shut down the slaughterhouse so we had to make our own."

"They do it because Grandpa did it." Kenneth parroted sadly. "You know, my parents didn't want me to quit my old job and try writing full-time. I don't usually tell people that in interviews. I say that they always supported me because I want kids to hear examples of supportive, loving parents. Really, they wanted me to stay with the family business too, a law firm. Just remember. What your folks did before you doesn't decide who you have to be."

***

John Opalenik

By the time the meat from his publicist that we didn't get to went bad, Kenneth had started teaching me the alphabet and what letters made which sounds after he'd realized how quickly I memorized the words of his book. I tried to focus on what he showed me and how I could apply it to any book, but I couldn't stop thinking about the fact that within days, we'd start carving pieces off him. Nobody had ever gotten away from us, and I'd been raised to believe that if anyone ever did, we'd all be dead before long, but I couldn't help but think that Kenneth belonged out in that world that he described to me through story and not in the dark stone basement, slowly disappearing piece by piece. "If you got away from this place, would you take me with you?"

He didn't cry or beg like others had when they thought I might be able to help them escape. Instead, he thought for a long time. "If I got away, I would send help back. If you were with me and the others caught me, they'd know you helped, and…they'd hurt you."

I didn't want to give up on the idea of him taking me into the other world. "If they caught up to you, you could act like you took me hostage, pretend to threaten me if they don't let you go."

"Elijah. I hate to say this, because I'm sure they mean something to you, but I'm not sure they'd care if someone threatened to hurt you." He sighed, half with the resignation of signing his own death warrant and half with the knowledge that what he said might hurt me.

C is for Chainsaw

"If you got away and sent help back here, wouldn't they think I'm just like Titus and Spike?" I hesitated to say it, "I mean…I am like them, but–"

"Don't say that, Elijah." Kenneth reached out and grabbed my shoulders. I winced, preparing for a strike since that's what Titus would have done, but the strike never came. "You're not like them, and once you get out of here, you don't have to act like them anymore. You're a victim, just like me and the others. The only difference is that you're going to get out of here."

A tear I barely understood fell down my cheek, leaving a clean streak on my dirty face. "So are you. I promise."

***

I drew a map of the area around the cabin and realized that my world was limited to a three-mile radius. I pointed out the areas that I thought were important. The river to the north and the road to the south were the most obvious ways to escape. Others have tried to hike through the woods east or west, but that never works. Nobody knows these woods like Titus. He knows anywhere someone might think to hide, and every way a person might try to escape.

I thought that sharing some of these would help Kenneth escape. I told him about the cliffs to the east where the river becomes a waterfall and the forest drops down onto harsh, unforgiving rocks before continuing further downstream. I told him that a patch of thornbushes gets so thick to the west that even the most desperate person can't force their way through. When he asked about the road and all the cars hidden under tarps outside the cabin, I told him that Spike removed at least one vital part from each of them, and even if someone could get a car on the road, his tow truck was souped up with an old stock car engine, and he'd run them off the road with ease.

"Kenneth. I'm not saying you shouldn't try to get away, but if they catch you again…don't let them catch you again."

"They aren't going to catch me again." He did his best to sound confident, but the lump in his throat was as obvious as the bloodstains on the floor.

"If someone tries to get away and they get caught, the first thing Titus does is take one leg from the knee down, tear out the bone, and cook it like a tenderloin." I look down, ashamed that Kenneth knows I've had many such meals. "He does it to scare people into staying put and to make it even harder to get away if they try something else."

"I know we've only got one shot at this, kid." Then he lied with the love of a parent. "It's going to be okay."

He told me he'd have a plan by morning and that I should get back upstairs so nobody would ask why I'd been spending so much time in the basement. I looked around the living room, with lampshades made of skin and wind chimes made from bones. Looked out our window into the forest and took a moment to appreciate that when winter is on its way,

14

you can see so much further into the green, and I couldn't help but wonder if some part of me would miss the only life I've known if I were to leave it all behind. I spent so much time thinking about how soft and pleasant the outside world seems to be, but until that moment, I never wondered if that world would even have someone like me.

***

When I returned to give him his breakfast and empty his shit bucket the next morning he told me his plan, or rather, the part of his plan that he knew I'd be willing to go along with. He asked me where we kept the matches to start the fireplace and told me that when the fire started I should climb down the cliffs since the roots and loose rocks would support my weight but nobody else's and escape downriver. He said that he'd use the distraction of the fire to escape in another direction and that he'd find me in whatever town the river led to first.

I'd been there when people tried to escape and might have even had an hour or two of freedom before Titus and Spike dragged them back into the house. They always tried to give themselves a head start by going in the middle of the night, or when they thought the weather would be on their side. This plan had the high risk of essentially announcing that something was going on, but making it almost impossible to ignore the fact that our little kingdom of pain was in flames.

I spent the next day quietly packing my bag of what few personal belongings from my old life I wanted to bring into my new one, along with practicalities. I put the money I'd been able to scrounge from the wallets of our victims over the years along with my copy of Kenneth's book into a plastic shopping bag to keep the paper safe from the river, snuck downstairs to give Kenneth the key to his shackles.

He rubbed the chafed skin on his wrist and we had what would end up being our final conversation.

"Kid, do you remember your mother?"

At the time, I didn't realize why he asked me that. "Titus always told me that they found me abandoned as a baby, that I would have frozen in the forest if it wasn't for him."

"I hate to say this because I know it might hurt you, but I think you need to know it before you go back into the world." Kenneth rested his big palm on my skinny shoulder. "There's no way Titus and the other one could keep a baby alive in this place. They had to have taken you as a young kid when they…did what they do, to your parents and maybe any siblings you might have had."

I didn't want to believe it because it would mean that I'd been living with my real family's murderers, and maybe even ate them. "If that's what happened, then why did they keep me?"

"You said that they have to keep us alive until they're ready to eat, except in winter." Kenneth struggled to imagine what dark thoughts went through Titus's twisted mind. "Maybe by the time they went through the rest of the meat…the rest of your real family, they'd gotten used to having you around. Maybe in a strange way, they started to see you as one of their own. Maybe Titus saw you as a way for his legacy to carry on after he's gone."

My eyes welled up with tears when I knew that what he was saying was true and that my existence all these years was even sicker than I thought. I wanted something of what I'd lost back. "Will you help me find them, if there's anybody left?"

"Just remember, Elijah. This isn't your fault. It was forced on you, just like it was on me. Remember that when you worry that you don't deserve the good that the world is going to offer you." He sent me away without saying goodbye.

I went upstairs and waited for the smell of smoke.

I noticed the smell before Titus or Spike could. Spike was outside working on his truck and Titus's once keen sense of smell had been dulled by decades of smoking and breathing in woodsmoke. Since the fireplace on the northwestern side of the house would be the first place one would look for a suspicious smoky smell, I crept out the window on the eastern side of the cabin, next to the coffee table full of bones sat between a couch and a chair with years of stains and ripped cushions.

As I strapped on the life jacket I'd taken from some poor dead kayaker and dyed it brown with caked-on mud and put on the backpack full of what few artifacts from my old life I took with me, I took one last look inside, I saw Kenneth digging through the kitchen cabinets until he found two knives with curved blades that, through the eyes of a child, looked more like swords. It didn't make me suspect anything at first. Anyone so keenly aware that they may be dragged back into our house of horrors would look for the hardware necessary to either go down swinging or take the easy way out. I'd told Kenneth what we do to the people who tried to escape and failed. The more and more certain doom as a person disappears piece by piece does something to their mind that I don't want to even think about happening to someone like Kenneth. I don't know if it was the determined look in his eyes when he turned away from the front door, or the acrid smell of propane hitting my nose that worked as my one warning of Kenneth's benevolent betrayal.

I thought about pleading with Kenneth to come with me, but when Titus came downstairs with a hammer gripped in his right hand, I knew there'd be no getting him out unless by some miracle he was able to take on both Titus and Spike. I began regretfully sneaking away as a combat between the only two father figures I'd ever known raged in the burning cabin, but when I heard Titus call out for Spike and he came running, I broke into a sprint, knowing that this would be my one chance to make it to the cliffs before someone took the time to notice me.

The map of the forest was burned into my mind for as long as I could remember, and as such, I was able to avoid the roots and loose rocks that gave many escapees the death sentence of a broken ankle over the years. I slowed when the cliff's edge came into view, suddenly about to go further from home than I'd ever gone before.

I lowered myself over the edge and took one last look at the burning cabin. The part of me still tethered to that old life the way others had been chained to the wall started to think of reasons to go back. Kenneth would need my help. They all would. I was the only one who knew there were people out here. Nobody else would come for them.

Before I could think too much about going back, I heard a loud explosion and a corner of the house blasted away. One of the propane tanks Spike stole from grills when he was on the road at night must have ignited. My whole body jolted when I flinched and I slipped off the wet root I'd been using as a foothold. I don't remember landing in the water, but by the time I came to, I'd been drifting downstream for hours, maybe days.

I knew I couldn't just float to the next town relying solely on my life jacket and brief excursions into the forest to forage, so I waited for an opportunity. Eventually, I found a house by the lake with a little raft, meant to be a child's pool toy next to a few kayaks meant for the people in the house. The afternoon sun illuminated the dock and the house bustled with activity, so I hid in the trees on the edge of their property and waited for my opportunity.

After a day of watching a family barbeque, teetering back and forth between curiosity and jealous rage, the sun set, the guests left, and the family turned off the lights. I waited another hour for them to fall asleep and made my move.

Throughout the party, they left the side door to the garage unlocked and people would walk in empty-handed and leave with food and drink, so I assumed they had food in there. Inside, I found myself surrounded by a pegboard wall full of power tools, saws, and other tools meant to build that I'd seen used for more nefarious purposes. Thinking back on it, the healthy reaction would have been to suffer a panic attack. Instead, I thought about which weapon I'd be best with if I had to fend off a wounded Titus or Spike trying to bring me back to the cabin. I settled on a box cutter with a retractable blade. Small enough to keep with me at all times, but with a razor's edge that could shred the flesh and tendons of anyone who tried to take me away.

Next, I saw two coolers and in the middle, a tall white box that I now recognize as a refrigerator. Within half an hour, I ate half a rotisserie chicken, and enough side dishes to leave my stomach bloated and full. I found a small cooler filled with beer. I spilled it all out once I noticed the familiar smell that often lingered on Spike's breath, filled it with whatever food I could fit, and snuck back down to the docks. One of the kayaks seemed like the obvious choice since it would get me downriver faster, but instead, I took the children's raft since I could sleep in it, and if I needed to, I could sink it with one slash of my box cutter.

C is for Chainsaw

I floated until I lost track of days and my supplies dwindled. When I encountered people and small towns I hid and continued under the cover of night. I know Kenneth told me to stop in the next town, but none of the ones I floated through at first were big enough to be anonymous within. When signs of civilization became more frequent, I took my copy of Kenneth's book and half the money I stashed away, and I put it in the cooler, which I then buried in a patch of forest that I'd be able to find again, but wouldn't be stumbled upon by anyone else. Then I sank the raft and wandered into a town and waited for someone to notice me.

Despite filling my head with a lot of harmful things, some of what Titus and Spike taught me came in handy. For one, they said never to tell the police the truth. So when a uniformed police officer asked where my parents were, I didn't say they'd been eaten in a cabin that burned down upriver. Instead, I thought about Kenneth's lie and how it had the marrow of truth in its bones.

I told her that I didn't know where my parents were and that a man took me away from them. I knew that she and her superiors would want details, and the same way we made a few pieces of meat last a whole winter, I rationed out details giving as little as I needed to in order to keep them from posting "missing child" posters with my face on it all over the county. I told them that I got away from the people who took me by hiding in the woods. I said I didn't remember my last name, and that they killed my parents and kept me for a long time. Those details were true.

When they asked where they'd kept me, I lied. I said that they moved around a lot, never staying in one place for more than a week. The final truth I told them that I hoped would keep them from making my whereabouts known to anyone from the cabin was that I was afraid that the people who took me would try to find me again.

It took a long time and a lot of trust, but after a year with a foster family, I was able to trick my new parents into thinking I was staying over at a friend's house and I went back to where I'd buried my copy of Kenneth's book. Then I ventured upriver and stealthily crept up to the old cabin.

It had burned down to its foundation and while there were the charred bones of countless victims strewn about, I only found two skeletons intact. I looked through the wreckage and saw that Spike's big souped-up truck was nowhere to be found. In the aftermath of what happened, he left the cabin and those woods behind the same as I did, but I'm certain he had no intention of beginning a new life.

Perhaps he sought out a new patch of secluded forest to build a new house of horrors. Maybe he took what skills he had and continued it on the road, more of a hunter than a trapper now. But the one scenario that kept me up at night was that one day, I would look out my new parents' window and I'd see that old truck parked across the street waiting to devour the new life I'd found and trap me within the burnt wreckage of my old one.

C is for Chainsaw

That's why I applied to colleges overseas, despite my parents' worries. That's why I'm going to burn this essay and write whatever essay I have to in order to get in and completely sever myself from the land where the bones of my old life are buried.

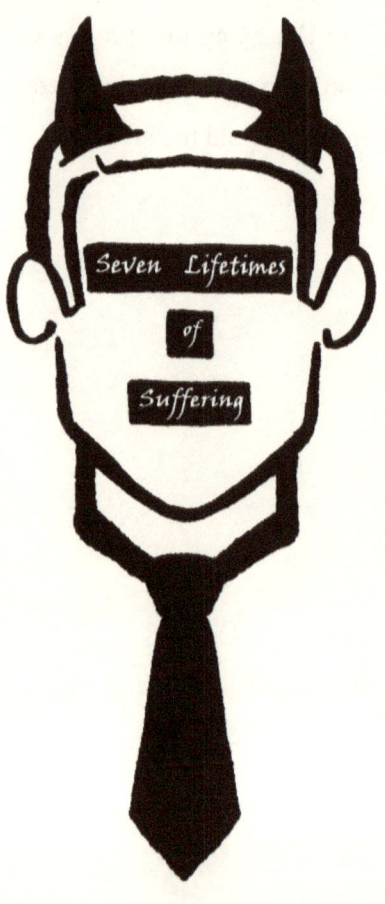

I'm having one of those days where if something bad can happen, it will. I couldn't hear my alarm over the wails of the damned, so I overslept. Then, when I went to look at my watch with the mug still in my hand, I spilled coffee over my last clean shirt. So after I went in the hamper and found the least dirty one, I got on the road. I'll admit, it's not a great neighborhood, hence the screaming of the damned, but apartments next to the Fields of Despair are all an entry-level demon like me can afford. It was either that or move back in with my parents, and that would be torturous even for Hell.

I walk into Mr. Evilian's office and see everything I hope I can be if I keep my head down and do the work. He has a corner office overlooking the Citadel of Torment. His designer suit has been tailored to allow room for his tail and all of the spines protruding from his shoulders and elbows. His horns are that of a ram, like mine, except somehow his hair is always perfectly styled and mine is a shaggy permanent bedhead due to my inability to work around the horns. One look at him and you get the feeling that he's a demon that has everything he wants.

"Sorry I'm late, Mr. Evilian. There was flooding on the River of Fire, so I had to take a detour." If it weren't for my red skin tone, he'd see me blushing as I sit down, open my briefcase, and hope my files are in order.

"Survive in this company long enough, and you'll know that the River of Fire always floods this time of year." Mr. Evilian growls. "Regardless, let's start your end-of-century review. Your file says you're Jacob Renderman, living on the second layer of Hell, interning here in the multi-lifetime karmic punishment department, hoping for a permanent position."

"That's right," I say, trying to sound eager. "I know I'm just eighty-five years in, but I'm hoping that by the time my two-hundred-year internship is done, I'll have earned my place here."

"Right. Well, we can start by looking at this. Soul number nine trillion seven hundred eighty-one billion, seven hundred thirty-three million, three hundred seventeen thousand, seven hundred two was sentenced to seven lifetimes of suffering for causing a ripple effect of bigotry and violence during one of his reincarnations last century. His suffering was your job." Mr. Evilian's brow furrows as much as it can between the horns. "I hate to say this, but it looks like you've been going easy on him."

I'm wounded by the accusation. I rifle through my paperwork to find something that would point out the contrary. "What about this? Three incarnations ago, I gave him a terminal illness."

Mr. Evilian scoffs. "You gave it to him in his late eighties. He died peacefully in a hospital surrounded by his loved ones. He had a long, full life by human standards."

I can't help but appear clueless. "Wait. How long do humans live again?"

Seven Lifetimes of Suffering

Mr. Evilian shakes his head dismissively. "At least you had the forethought to make sure he died before knowing that his grandson had gotten engaged, but still. There wasn't nearly enough suffering."

"I–I thought," I stammer.

"You can get away with that sort of thing if you're particularly brutal in their next life, but it says here that you didn't do anything to him the following reincarnation." Mr. Evilian looks like he's deciding whether or not to do something. I hope it's something like taking me on as a protégé, but he could just as easily be deciding whether or not to terminate my internship early.

"To be fair," I hesitate, wondering if I should just apologize and do better, or assert myself. I decide that Mr. Evilian would assert himself, and so I do the same. Nobody gets anywhere in Hell without being a little prideful. "He was reincarnated as a tree. It's not like I had a lot to work with. Besides, I didn't count that as one of his seven lifetimes of suffering. If Susan in accounting counted that, I'd say that's on her."

Mr. Evilian looks surprised, maybe even impressed. "You know what? Fuck it." He puts my paperwork back in the filing cabinet. "I'm going to do for you what someone did for me a few millennia ago when I was an entry-level demon just trying to get my hoof in the door."

I try to look intrigued rather than eager. "What's that?"

"I'm going to take you out to lunch. You have the length of one meal to impress me. Either way, you're coming back here and cleaning out your fucking desk." He looks greedily thrilled, like someone who just placed a high-stakes bet. "Because Monday you're either going to be shoveling shit in the Valley of the Grotesque, or you'll be setting up your office right down the hall from mine."

***

We get in his convertible and he speeds down the highway to the fifth level of Hell. I've never even been past the third, and that was just for work. Mr. Evilian's smirk widens to make him look extra carnivorous. He's clearly enjoying the novelty of someone being so impressed with what he might have been taking for granted for centuries. "What are you in the mood for? I know a steakhouse where they carve the meat off the sinner right at the table."

"Sounds noisy." I wave my hand dismissively. "If we're going to talk business, we need to eat somewhere that we can actually have a conversation."

"I like the way you think, kid." He shifts into a higher gear and lets the engine roar. "I know a nice seaside place where the only noise is the sound of waves of boiling blood crashing."

We get right into the restaurant and I suddenly realize that simply saying that I'm going to deliver the seven lifetimes of suffering isn't going to be enough. I'd already fucked that up. My only chance of ever being more than just an entry-level demon intern is to say something that's never been said, and if he gives me a chance, I have to fucking deliver.

"What are you drinking?" I head to the bar fully aware that I need a shot of confidence.

"Doesn't matter. I just need something to take the edge off." I hesitate. "I'm about to make a big proposal to my boss and it's all or nothing."

"I've got what you need." The bartender pours a shot of whiskey and brings out a tray of vials filled with a dark red liquid. "Add a couple drops of serial killer blood and it'll give a demon all the confidence he needs."

"Dahmer…Gacy…There's no way I could afford any of that!" I step back as if he'd charge me for even getting a whiff of it.

"Maybe not now." He puts a few drops from another vial into the shot glass. "But if things work out for you, just remember who your friends are." He slides the shot my way and pours another for himself. "Here's to bold moves and big payouts."

***

I head back to the table where Mr. Evilian is sucking the marrow from a freshly cracked femur the way someone on Earth would crack a lobster and devour its meat. "Okay, kid. Impress me."

"They've got this saying up on Earth, that hurt people hurt people." Evilian looks a little disgusted that I pay that much attention to what a human has to say, but he lets me continue. "If that's the case, then we don't need to collect our debts right away. Just plant little seeds of pain that will lead to even bigger payouts when we finally collect. Think about soul number 9,781,733,317,702. Who gives a shit that I didn't give it some weird fungal infestation when it reincarnated as a tree? It's more of a chore on our end and what does it really get us? Nothing. If we prod with little punishments once in a while, it'll make them feel justified in their transgressions more and more until they've fattened up enough. Then we'll hit them so hard that seven lifetimes of suffering will feel like nothing."

Mr. Evilian considers as he gets the last bit of marrow from the bone. "I understand your idea, but do you really think the execs on the deeper levels of Hell will want us taking our foot off the gas?" He looks up, considering the angles. "It's risky, and I've done too much to stick my neck out just to have a chance to make it to an office a few levels deeper."

My first instinct is to back down, but then I think about working a manual labor job in the Valley of the Grotesque, and realize that I've said too much to back out now. "That's the thing. If we do this right, we can sell it to everyone in charge. The ones down on the sixth and seventh levels don't care about the minutiae of end-of-century reviews. They look at a whole millennium at least. Even the guys upstairs will get behind it."

Seven Lifetimes of Suffering

Mr. Evilain shudders at the thought of angels thinking about his performance reviews. "What makes you think they care what we do?"

I gesture to the stumps of old wings, sharpened into spines on Mr. Evilian's back. "We were all colleagues once. They might be the carrot, and we might be the stick, but at the end of the day, we have similar goals. They might actually like the optics of it. Less injustices for the reincarnations that don't appear to deserve it at the time. Their PR department won't have to go around saying that He works in mysterious ways as often, and we can focus on getting shit done. Everybody wins."

I can tell Mr. Evilian wants to regain some of his dominance after the thought of angels made him flinch. "What's to stop me from burying you in the Valley of the Grotesque and taking your ideas for yourself?"

"You said it yourself. You aren't willing to stick your neck out for it." I stand up confidently to make him feel like I could be his equal. "Clearly, I am. Send me out with the idea, and back me when I need it, and you get half the reward but none of the risk. Nobody's going to give you a better deal than that."

He picks his teeth with a splinter of bone. "You're right about that. Nobody from middle management is willing to collaborate the way you are. That's why all they do is maintain the status quo…" He tosses the shard of bone into the red plastic basket. "Fuck it. Go back to the office, pack your shit, and get Helen in HR to have someone make up a nameplate for your new office, the one right next to mine."

***

A month later I'm looking out the window of my new office overlooking the Citadel of Torment but not seeing the obsidian tower of suffering everyone else sees when they look at it. I look at it and see luxury apartments, designer suits, secret meetings between the top demonic executives and the angels we'll have managed to impress. I see a climb to the top and the tormented remains of whoever gets between me and where I want to be.

Our friends crowd around me at the back of the funeral home and mumble that Ada's parents should have let me stand up by the casket as the endless procession of family and half-forgotten friends filed in and gave their generic condolences. I tell them that I don't need to hear, "I'm sorry for your loss" dozens of times while standing there with my arms crossed. It wouldn't honor Ada or help me process the cruelty and randomness of her death. I probably don't convince them and I definitely don't convince myself.

Truthfully, I just can't bring myself to stand next to her open casket knowing that while the funeral home made her look peaceful from the waist up, there's no way they were able to undo the damage done when

33

the sedan mounted the curb and rolled over Ada as she walked our dog after work, crushing her legs and causing her femur to snap and sever her femoral artery. They can't replace the blood that dripped down the side of the road and into the storm drain as she dragged herself ten yards toward our house before her body gave out. No funeral home can dislodge the permanent lump in my throat that formed when I found her, minutes too late to even comfort her.

I can't stand next to the lie of her remains and not think about how whoever hit her simply drove home, washed her blood off their windshield with a garden hose, and simply moved on with their lives in a way I know I never will.

The procession moves from the funeral home to the cemetery where I expect them to put her in the hole in the ground beside her grandparents, but instead, they just leave the casket next to the grave and wait for everyone to leave. From there, the groups of people who occupied different parts of Ada's life split up and either go home or find somewhere meaningful to raise a glass in her honor. That's what we do. Getting drinks at The Spigot, her favorite dive bar, is the last thing I want to do, but I go anyway. I know that if I opt out, Matty, Quinn, Corinne, and Sabrina, our core group of friends, would insist they go back to the house with me, reasoning that I shouldn't be alone. Besides the Xannax they gave me to fend off a panic attack at the funeral feels like it's wearing off and there's no way I can face tonight sober.

Haunt Me Forever

Matty insists he buys my drinks tonight. "It's the least I can do, Brian. The last thing you need to worry about on a night like tonight is the bar tab."

The way he and Corinne make concerned eye contact each time he buys a round makes me think that the only reason he offered was so he could keep track of how much I've had to drink. It doesn't work. I order whiskey shots each time I excuse myself to go to the bathroom, and by the time there's more of a crowd, I have to go into the stall and prepare to either shit, throw up, or sob. I stop to take a breath halfway through doing the latter two and decide to go to the sink and splash water on my face. When I look up, I see my faded reflection in the metal of the paper towel dispenser, and amidst the tags written in Sharpie and band stickers stuck to the walls, I see a black sticker that looks new. It must be a death metal band because above the image of an Ouija board, the band's name stares back at me in the illegible font that looks like something between a lightning bolt and a wound, popular among such bands. When I look back into the distorted reflection of my eyes, I see an equally misshapen figure standing behind me, looking as if she were reading over my shoulder. It has Ada's heart-shaped face with her dark hair up in a messy bun, but instead of the green eyes that looked even brighter when we went to Elizabeth Park in the spring, they are a pale mint green, almost as if the color drained from her eyes along with the blood from her body.

John Opalenik

I turn around only to find a tile wall covered in stickers and drawings of dicks. I turn back and look to see if she's still in the reflection. She isn't, but the sticker with the Ouija board on it stares back at me. At that moment, I don't care about every cautionary tale that Corinne and Sabrina share with their love of spooky shit. I decide that I'm going to find a way to see Ada, talk to her, or at least say goodbye.

When it gets late enough, a new generation of college kids arrives to make us thirty-somethings feel as out of place as we look in our funeral attire. Nobody asks if I'm good to drive, because none of us are. Sabrina's husband picks up the girls and Matty and Quinn split an Uber. They offer to drop me off home, but I tell them that the ten-minute walk home actually sounds kind of nice. The real reason I want the peace and quiet of a walk is that I want to figure out the first steps of my plan before I get home and pass out.

I furiously Google all the ways people have tried to speak to the dead over the years. I don't care about warnings that they've been debunked or that people have ended up haunted. That's the thing: I want to be haunted. I jot down a list in my notes app, and when I find out that people have developed apps meant to help people speak to ghosts, I download all of them. I'm sure most of them are designed to scare kids at sleepover parties, but if even one of the countless ways I reach out works, it will have been worth it.

Haunt Me Forever

The next morning, I wake up with my phone open to an app claiming to be the number one real ghost detecting app on the market set to detect, amplify, and record any EVPs. A quick Google search reveals that an EVP is an electronic voice phenomenon, essentially, ghost voices caught on a recording. My tablet has another app open claiming to detect shifts in electromagnetic fields. The TV is playing a YouTube video playing ambient sound which is apparently at a frequency that opens the listener up to the other side.

An entire notebook is filled with pages that are either scribbled into oblivion or have gibberish written across them. I assume that I tried my hand at automatic writing. According to the apps and the ruined notebook, my drunken one-man seance amounted to nothing. I can't let that stop me. If it were that easy, everyone would do it. I come up with a list of excuses for why it didn't work. First of all, I need to continue casting a wide net, get every spirit communication tool from any religion or New Age set of beliefs, and do it all at once. I'm not like those ghost-hunting shows where I'm trying to either prove that it works or that the skeptics are right. I don't care what anyone else believes. I just have to find a way to talk to Ada again.

My bereavement leave gives me enough free time while my friends and family are working to go to a metaphysical shop a few towns over and ask for every tool or resource to speak with the dead. The woman running the shop somehow looks retro and trendy at the same time, with the light flowy clothing of a hippie, but with the tattoos, piercings, and mullet-esque hairstyle recently resurrected by twenty-somethings.

"Welcome to A Look Beyond. I'm Sage. Are you just browsing or is there something specific I can help you with?"

I glance around at the arrangements of books, crystals, pendulums, and other things I couldn't name if I tried. "Yeah. I wouldn't know where to start. I made a list." I hand it to her and her shoulders drop as she connects the dots and realizes what I'm trying to do. She looks into my eyes with a sad pleading look that mirrors a fraction of my anguish.

She quickly collects the more benign items like incense and crystals said to clear a space and make communication with a spirit easier. When I try to buy things that come with warnings online like spirit boxes and Ouija boards, she hesitates but ultimately puts them on the counter next to the register. When she gives me a total, I give her my credit card and she pauses as if searching for the right words before taking it. "There's a lot of stuff here that I'm guessing you've never used before…" Her voice trails off as she considers leaving it at that. "Just make sure you read all the instructions and do your research before using it."

I thank her and take the bag out of the store quickly. I know that if I linger, then the unspoken understanding we share may cause me to hesitate and my determination to talk to Ada again could melt into a more mundane mourning which would mean an end without a goodbye.

Haunt Me Forever

Over the next two nights, I put everything where I'm told I should to open communication between worlds, and I try new ways to reach out. Some run in the background like the apps searching for EVPs, but others I need to engage with. The plan is to try at least a few new things each night until something works. I remember a conversation about how Ada once pretended to get sick and left a sleepover party when she was a teenager because the other girls took out a Ouija board, so I save that for last, hoping that she'll make herself known to me before I have to try something that scared her.

I try my hand at automatic writing again, scribbling my hand across notebook pages and hoping an unseen force would guide my hand and write me a message from Ada. It makes me realize how we used to exchange dozens of texts a week and completely took them for granted. Now I'd do just about anything for one such message.

Another night passes and this time it's raining, not the gentle mist that came the night a random driver hit Ada and didn't bother to stop or even call someone. Tonight, it's a real downpour that forces all but the most determined to stay inside.

A knock from upstairs makes me drop the planchette I was just about to put to use. Instead, I follow the soft, but persistent percussion up toward our bedroom.

"Ada." I don't feel nearly as self-conscious as I thought I would when I call out to her in an empty house. "Are you there?"

A louder knock and the sound of something dragging across a wooden surface.

"That's good. Keep knocking so I can find you." My voice catches in my throat. "Ada, I've missed you so much."

By the time I get upstairs, I realize that the knocking is coming from the attic.

When I go downstairs to get a step stool so I can reach the hatchway, the banging intensifies and starts coming in patterns. For the briefest moment I consider that she may be trying to reach out with Morse Code, but then I realize that if she didn't know Morse Code in life, why the hell would she in death?

My front door creeps open and I see a figure silhouetted by the streetlight behind her. At first, I assume it's Ada, because who else could it be? But as soon as she steps inside I see that instead of the dark messy bun and heart-shaped face of a ghostly Ada that I expected to see, I see the round face and unruly curls of Sage, wearing flannel pajama bottoms, and a tank top instead of the New Age hippie witchy aesthetic that she had back at her shop. At first, I wonder why she's here, how she found my address and a dozen other questions, but the only one that passes my lips is the most foolish and pointless of all. "Why are you barefoot?"

She rushes forward with a jerky motion and grabs me by the shoulders, partly to catch herself from falling and partly to get my attention. "Brian! You have to get out of here." Her eyes look more green than the hazel ones I remember from the store, and the way her mouth moves, when she speaks it looks like she isn't quite sure how to move. "You aren't safe."

"Are you okay? You look like you got hurt or something. Why are you here? What do you mean I'm not safe?"

"Look. She's like a foot shorter than I was and her face feels funny. I'm just not used to it. Just get out of the house and I'll explain everything."

The door slams behind her, which I should find alarming, but instead I notice all the little details. The height difference, the hint of New Jersey in her accent, the way she says my name. Then I realize.

"Ada." I fall to my knees, lightheaded and overwhelmed at finally getting what I wanted.

"Brian! You aren't safe." She tries to pick me up, but we both end up in a half crouch when the banging sound upstairs turns into a crash and a sound of broken glass. "You opened every door to the other side and didn't think for a second about what else might come through. That's not me upstairs. It's something else."

We rush hand-in-hand for the door, and when it's locked we look at the stairs. I pause and look at Ada's eyes on Sage's face. "If I opened every door, why didn't you come back to me until now?"

"I can't haunt you forever. I have to go to the other side so you can move on and live your life. If I came back it wouldn't have been just to

41

say goodbye. We'd have lingered, haunting each other, putting your life and my afterlife on hold. We'd be stuck in the in-between place where there are other things that aren't safe for either of us."

The sounds of destruction upstairs intensify and then stop.

"Things like that."

A shadow made of liquid with limbs like a centipede creeps down the stairs, and onto the ceiling above us. It gets bigger and stronger as it gets closer to us, nourished by our pain. It reaches out, but Ada grabs my wrist and pulls me out of the way. We go up to the bedroom we shared and shove the bed in front of the heavy old wooden door.

"What are we supposed to do?" I ask, hoping Ada learned something in her brief tenure as a ghost.

She looks down at the body she's wearing. "I used her to get here because I thought she might know." She blinks and I see Sage's hazel eyes again, and she recoils at the sight of me. "What's going on? How did I get here? Are you going to hurt me?"

I do my best to explain the trouble we're in quickly and as soon as she considers not believing a word of it, the lights flicker out and the banging at the door resumes. "Sage. What do we do?"

"It's feeding off your pain, your loss, and Ada's too. I can't make that go away, but maybe the two of you can." Her eyes roll back into her head and I see Ada's green eyes again.

"The only way this thing doesn't feed on our souls is if we get over this loss. How do we do that before it breaks down the door? How do we do that in a lifetime?"

Ada touches my cheek and presses her forehead to mine. "We have to remember what feels impossible when we lose someone. This isn't the end. We don't end. Nothing does."

We drop to our knees, foreheads touching with our fingers laced behind each other's necks. "I'll see you again."

The sound of the house coming apart around us stops. The silence is more peaceful than it has any right to be. When I look up, Ada isn't there anymore. Instead, Sage looks at me wondering if we're safe.

"It's okay. We're going to be okay."

"What happened?"

"I had to realize that Ada will haunt me for the rest of my life, but not forever."

Every cul-de-sac contains a secret or two, whether it's the loss of a job, an affair, or a darker story that remains untold outside the confines of its suburban context. This is one of those tales.

It all started when things started going missing from people's yards, unlocked garages, and toolsheds. People had their assumptions. Maybe the guy with the shopping cart full of cans who made the rounds every once in a while realized that he could do better than five cents a can. Perhaps the Anderson's son, Leon, was getting into drugs and needed the extension cords, grills, and power tools to pawn for quick cash. Some of us even had the simple theory that the suburbs were only a few miles from the city, and criminals had cars just like the rest of us.

Nobody protested when Claire Emrys proposed a neighborhood watch organization. She'd been a wreck looking for some sort of control over her life after her husband walked out on her and their son a few weeks earlier, leaving her a single mother of one with another on the

44

way. In fact, she'd been keeping her son in the house or away at her in-laws' house since Todd went missing.

Believe it or not, I was one of the first people to sign up for a shift. To be honest, I felt a little insecure after someone stole the propane tank off our grill. The idea that someone came onto our property and took something while I was home with Kimberly and little Ashley, and I didn't do anything to stop it, got under my skin. I usually didn't buy into the whole traditional gender roles tough guy act, but it made me feel helpless, like every time I got bullied as a kid.

I thought about breaking out the shotgun my grandfather left me, but Kimberly and I agreed that in order to have it ready to go at a moment's notice, we'd be putting our curious toddler, Ashley, in harm's way. Instead, I signed up for a karate class, which made me feel a little silly whenever I found myself walking into the dojo as a bunch of tweens walked out from the previous class, but the first time I knocked over the freestanding punching bag with a base full of water, I felt empowered that I might actually be able to do something if someone tried to break into our house.

I went out on my first patrol, which was really just walking our dog, Milo while keeping an eye on things at 11:00 at night and then going to bed right after. My first walk was uneventful, but I did notice some litter, including cans and bottles that the man with the shopping cart usually would have taken for himself. I also started to make note of who still had the lights on in their house in the middle of the night. The Anderson's house had its lights off except for the blue glow of a TV screen coming from one of the bedrooms.

For a while, it seemed like nothing would come of our nightly patrols until Leon Anderson went missing. He'd borrowed his mother's car to take a girl to the movies. The Andersons found the car on the side of the road just past the end of our street. If only he'd parked one house further down the road, whatever happened would have been caught on the Chapman's doorbell camera.

That's when I realized that if anyone went past the Chapman house, we'd have it recorded. I thought it would lead to a week of laboriously scrubbing through hours of footage, but thankfully their camera only starts recording when the motion sensor is set off, and on our little dead-end-road, we don't get a lot of traffic from people who don't live here. What few other cars we saw were just guests of one of us. Sure, someone could have snuck in through the woods behind each of our backyards, but I started thinking that whatever happened to Leon, and whatever other strange goings-on were occurring, it may have been one of our neighbors behind it.

When Todd took off, people were shocked, but the police never got involved. People walk out on their families. He didn't seem like the type, but stranger things have happened. This time, with Leon going missing and no obvious explanation, soon our little cul-de-sac was swarming with police.

Everyone got interviewed, houses were searched, and nothing came of it. The police eventually wrote it off, saying that he probably ran away from home. It didn't make sense to any of us, not because he had such a great relationship with his parents, but because he left his car, his money, and virtually all his belongings behind. After a week, the police left, but our paranoia remained.

The day before my next shift of neighborhood watch, Kimberly and I took Ashley around in the stroller, not just so we could get her some fresh air, but so we could take a hard look at our neighborhood. We noted where all of the doorbell cameras were, and Kimberly made me promise never to be out of view of one. We also agreed that I would bring a rescue whistle that I bought for my week-long solo hike through the Maine chunk of the Appalachian Trail. It was designed to be loud enough that anyone in the neighborhood could hear it. Our final precaution was that Kimberly said she'd wait up for me to make sure I came home on time.

The night of my next patrol came, and we walked up and down the street, making certain to stay within view of the various doorbell cameras. It led to a lot of awkward crisscrossing the street, and a few sprints through the blind spots, but nothing happened until we almost made it home. Bowie must have heard something, because she darted across the street and started sniffing at something by Claire Emry's side door. My first instinct was to call out, but when Claire opened the door waving a strip of fake bacon, which she knew was Bowie's favorite treat, I stood back. Why would she want my dog in her house? I looked back at my house, where the little life Kimberly and I had built waited for me, and across the street I saw an enigma possibly holding the secret to who or what had been silently threatening our peaceful little existence these past few weeks. With a blend of curiosity and protective instinct, I turned off my flashlight and crept toward Claire's house.

I peered through the kitchen window and ducked away quickly when I saw Claire leading Bowie into the basement. When she closed the door behind her, I looked more closely. Her typical suburban kitchen had been converted into an apocalypse bunker. Rather than a bowl of apples on the counter, there were cases of canned goods. Instead of a countertop full of appliances, there were camping supplies and jugs of water. I didn't know what was going on, but I knew that I had to find out. I circled around the back of the house and grabbed the spare key in the hollow garden gnome where she told me it was that week she, and Todd went to Block Island and she wanted me to feed her cat.

When I got inside, I noticed that they didn't have any bags of cat food or a litter box anymore. I found it hard to believe that Todd took the cat when he left, so I kept exploring, careful not to let my footsteps alert Claire to my presence. I noticed that none of Paul's toys were strewn about the living room as they'd been every time we ever went over to their house. When I walked by the doorway to Paul's room, it was empty. No bed. No school supplies. Nothing. When Todd left, he hadn't packed a U-Haul. He didn't even say he was leaving. There was no way he somehow moved all of Paul's stuff out. Claire didn't even say that Paul was gone. She said he was homesick, or spending time at his grandparents' house. I walked into the house with questions, and everything I found only added more mysteries, and all of the answers were in the basement with Claire and Bowie.

I did my best to be stealthy, and not let the wooden steps creak. I saw Claire tighten a doggie backpack with a length of rope fastened to it to Bowie and then she pointed to a doorway with more stairs leading downward. When Bowie didn't go, she threw the remainder of the dog treats down, and off she went.

That's when Claire noticed me.

"You shouldn't be here, Tom."

"What are you doing, Claire? What happened to you?"

Her vulnerability began to show, with weeks off a tough exterior beginning to crack. "What would you do to see the people you love most again?"

At first, I thought she was threatening to keep me in the basement. As long as she was unarmed, I knew I could get away. I decided to call her bluff. "Claire. You're very pregnant. There's no way you can stop me from leaving."

"That's just what's wrong with you people in this neighborhood. You think it's all about your precious, perfect little household. That's why I couldn't tell you what really happened."

"What happened?" I glanced over her shoulder at the stairwell heading down into darkness. "What's down those stairs? Where is Paul?"

She finally broke. "I don't know. He was the first one to see the stairs. They're only here for a few minutes at midnight each night. When he called us into the basement to show us, we thought it might be some tiny crawlspace that we never noticed when we bought the house, but then when he showed us, that…" she gestured to the ancient stone steps that appeared to be carved out of the bedrock upon which the house was built. "Then he went down the stairs and…the sound of his footsteps just kept going. There was no way it could go down that deep, but it did. Watch." She took a red ball and bounced it down the stairs. It bounced twice before I couldn't see it anymore but I heard at least two dozen more bounces, each more quiet than the last before it stopped, not because it hit the bottom, but because it was too far away to hear.

"Todd went down after him." It was a statement more than a question.

"When we called and called and got no reply, he had to. When neither of them came back, I wanted to follow them, but with a little girl on the way…" She cradled her eight-month pregnant abdomen. "Then I thought I could reel them in, kind of like fishing. First I used our thirty-foot extension cord for the Christmas lights, but that wasn't enough. Then, the next day, I bought a hundred feet of rope. I tossed that down and pulled it back so many times before it came back with a note attached to it."

"A note?"

"I always thought Todd was such a dork for keeping a pen in his pocket all the time, but I guess it finally came in handy. He wrote it on the only paper he had." She handed me a folded-up dollar bill with, "Nothing alive can come back up. Send food. Love you." written on it.

"That's when you started sending down the canned goods and all of Paul's stuff." I thought about what I would do if Ashley were stuck somewhere and all I could do was send her supplies. "Is that where Leon went?"

"When Todd said that nothing alive can come back, I wanted to give him...more material to work with. At first, it was stray cats, but then I thought that maybe animals aren't the same as people. Next, I sent down that guy with the shopping cart full of cans, and then Leon. Nothing has worked."

"Why did you give them our dog?"

"If they're stuck down there, I don't want him to feel alone. He has his father and the others, but," she held her face in her hands, tears running between her fingertips. "He always wanted a dog."

"Why didn't you tell someone? Why do all this?"

51

"I was afraid. Afraid that the police would show up and the door would never reappear. Afraid that I made it all up or that I'm going crazy. Afraid that I'd be blamed for what happened and they'd take my little girl away when she's born." She reached out to me with her tear-drenched hands. "You have to keep my secret, or I'll never see my little boy again."

"Where does this end, Claire?" I pulled away from her. "How can I know you won't put me or my family in danger to save them?"

"Give me one week." She pleaded. "If I don't get them back in one week, you can send tell whoever you want, let them take me away. I won't fight. Just please, give me one week."

***

I took Kimberly and Ashley up to Freeport, Maine for a week. I said it would be great to do some outlet shopping since Ashley was growing so fast, and it would be nice to get away with everything that had been going on in our neighborhood. When I came home, Paul, Todd, and Leon were back. They weren't the same as they were when they disappeared, but they were back. Nobody offered to tell me what happened to the guy with the shopping cart, and I didn't ask. Leon and his parents moved away from the neighborhood as quickly as they could sell their house, and we never heard from them again.

As for the Emrys family, they renovated their basement, and I even offered to help lay the bricks that made up the wall that locked away the

The Midnight Staircase

midnight staircase and kept anyone else from stumbling onto our cul-de-sac's dark secret.

I tell you. The strangest thing I ever seen in this here saloon was when a man who called himself Zachariah darkened the door during one of our nightly poker games, back when we had poker games at the saloon. It was a night not unlike this one, with a chill in the air hinting at the coming of the fall and the night coming earlier and earlier with each passing day. Sat around the poker table were four of our regulars.

There was Maxwell St. Germaine, a dude from back East who liked spending his family's money and playing at being the pioneering type. I think he knew better than anyone else that he was full of shit, but he didn't seem to mind. To his right, sat Garrett Wilson, a man who had done just about every job you could imagine in these parts at some time or another during the mere twenty-five years he'd walked this earth. Told me once that he'd even tried his hand at being a lawman. He said he could've been good at it, but it left a bad taste in his mouth. Then there was old Jasper O'Malley. He was an old-timer who spent his days in the creek panning for gold, and spent whatever he found just as quickly on whiskey and cards. Then there was Eli Paulson. He didn't know a damn thing about what cards were likely to be in someone's hand, but he had a talent for pissing people off and getting them to make stupid bets.

I've known some saloon owners who didn't want poker in their joint. They said it slowed the action in a place to a crawl, but in a small saloon like mine, with four tables and a few stools by the bar, it worked out just fine. If one of my four tables had half a dozen guys who kept buying drinks for hours on end, I'd do a good day's business regardless.

I almost forgot. Clem was there too and so was I, except we both had less gray hair back in them days. That was round abouts twenty years ago or more at this point. Back when young men would come into town and order their drinks from Clem rather than me, but they'd call her name out almost like a song. "Clementine." And they'd put as much honey in their voice as they could muster after a long ride on the trail into town. What I'm saying is, I ain't bullshitting you. Hand to God what I'm about to tell you really happened and if you don't believe me, just ask Clem.

It was a cold night, and we'd just gotten our first dusting of snow from the harsh winter that was to come. Maxwell, Garret, Eli, and Jasper were a few rounds into a poker game. If memory serves, I think Garret was winning, but I could be wrong. Garret's the kind of guy who looks like he's winning even when he ain't. Eli was talking shit, saying that if Garret was as good with women as he was with cards, he'd've given up the game by now. He said it with a sly grin though. That was Eli's game, saying things that'd make you drop your guard. Nobody paid it no mind, save for anyone who didn't know him. He was the sort of guy you'd swear was an unrepentant asshole until you got to know him. After that, you'd know that he'd give you the coat off his back in a blizzard if he considered you a friend. Anyway, Garret didn't fall for it, and he kept his money, at first.

Then he came in.

Man went by the name of Zachariah. Took him for some kind of a preacher or an outlaw at first, dressed as he was, all in black with the shadows keeping pace with his movement, both drawing your attention and not letting you get a full look at him. He bellied up to the bar and ordered a Kentucky bourbon. I couldn't quite place his accent, so I asked him if he was from out that way. He just said that he was from lots of places and he might've picked up a little of the Appalachian drawl along the way. He told me he'd just been dropped off by a wagon coming from back East and intended to spend the night in town before making arrangements for the next leg of his travels.

I think old Jasper was the first to notice him and saw the evidence of the money he might've had. Those black leather boots still had their shine and the tip of each toe had a shiny silver cap that looked like it'd been made from melted down coins. "Does the feller in the black suit want to play some cards while he drinks, or is he just resting his bones?" he asked.

I told him that he ought to ask the man himself, and he did straight away. Zachariah downed the rest of his whiskey and ordered another before he took a seat at the table with the boys. With a voice at once harsh and sweet, like honey whiskey, he thanked them for inviting him to their game and bought a round of drinks for the table. I should've seen trouble coming when he downed the extra drink in one gulp and he chuckled at Maxwell when he sipped at it slowly. He even egged on Eli to pile on the ridicule. "Damn, Maxwell, I don't even need to hear that Yankee accent to know you ain't from whiskey country. All I got to do is watch the way you sip your drink like it's your first."

Normally, Maxwell took it in stride when Eli poked fun at the fact that he came from a well-to-do family in New York, but for some reason, Maxwell took it personal this time. He ordered another drink and downed it in one swallow before raising his bet.

The night crawled on and the men kept drinking, talking, and playing cards. I noticed that the four regulars were putting up more money than they normally would. I didn't pay it no mind at first. It's wasn't any of my business, so long as they had enough left over to pay for their drinks. Normally there weren't any hard feelings in a game between regulars. They'd all be back next time with a determination to win back what they'd lost. Truly the only way the four could suffer a crushing defeat is if some cardshark were passing through just long enough to clean them out and leave forever with their money. Hell, that'd be a loss for me too, since the winnings wouldn't be spent at the bar. I kept an eye out for that, not that I could've done a damn thing about it, but Zachariah, clever as he seemed to be, wasn't winning so much as a hand. Either he was a bad card player, or he was just unlucky as all Hell.

None of the boys seemed to mind having Zachariah around. Every joke he cracked split their sides. They followed each suggestion he made without question.

"Oh, Clementine. Get us five steaks so bloody that we'd have to chase them down if they was any rarer." He had a bit of a song in his voice, but Clem always told me that something about it made her feel like a snake was crawling up her arm.

The guys didn't usually eat a full meal while playing cards, but Zachariah insisted on paying for it, so who was I to question it? When Clem got the steaks to the table, I've got to say, I was a little taken aback by the way Zachariah ate his. The way his suit was tailored and cleaned, I'd have thought that he'd tuck a handkerchief into his shirt to keep from making a mess, but I'd have been wrong about that. He cut up the meat into chunks big enough that I'd have choked on them, and he tore into them like a coyote tearing apart a jackrabbit. He was right when he said he liked his steak bloody, and I swear, if he wasn't clean-shaven, his beard would have been stained red from it.

***

There followed a few more hands, and I noticed that my regulars weren't playing like they was friends anymore. Sure, they always got in their jabs, sometimes just for a laugh or sometimes to trick a man into making a stupid bet. And yeah, sometimes it got out of hand, particularly when one or more of them's had a drink too many, but the worst it ever got was old Jasper would sit out the next few games and claim it was because he'd been spending more time in the creek panning for gold. Then he'd come back a week or two later like nothing ever happened. This didn't feel like that. You know that feeling in a room when you just know something bad's going to happen? I've been tending bar for the better part of thirty years and I've seen things go bad more than once…Anyway, that's the feeling I got.

Next thing you know, old Jasper called Garret's bluff and came out on top with three aces in his hand. Trouble was, there shouldn't have been three aces left in the deck. I wasn't sure at first, but Clem told me that from what she'd seen when she brought them their drinks, those cards had already been played. Anyway, Garret took that personally.

"You can't have had that hand," Garret shouted. "With what's been played so far, there ain't that many aces left in the deck."

"Yer the one cheatin!" Jasper countered. "How would you know how many aces should be left if you weren't cheating?"

"Paying attention ain't cheating." Garret slammed his fist on the table. "Just because you're too much of a God damned drunk to do it yourself don't make it cheating."

Zachariah stood up with a movement both lightning-fast and so smooth that the two men hardly noticed him until he positioned himself between them. "Easy, boys. The night is young. You'll have plenty of time to win that money back, Garret. That is, if you keep on playing. Can't win your money back from Jasper if he leaves the game with a broken nose."

"Prove that you ain't cheating," Garret demanded.

"Gentlemen, we can solve this quite simply. We can check the discarded cards and see if the aces have been played," Zachariah offered. "That is if everyone here agrees to it."

Jasper was the first to respond. "I'm fine with it. Go ahead and prove I ain't cheatin."

"We'll see about that," Garret growled.

"Well shit. Go ahead and check so they can get back to losing their money to me." Eli added, unable to hold back an opportunity to twist the knife a bit.

"I suppose if it will diffuse the situation, I'm game," Maxwell added.

Hooves

Zachariah slowly went through the deck, thoughtfully making sure each man could see every card as he went. When all was said and done, the aces Garret expected to see weren't there and it looked like old Jasper was right.

"Well shit," Garret's jaw dropped open. "I could've sworn some of those cards had already been played."

"I don't mean to offend," Zachariah placed a hand on Garret's shoulder like a father trying to console a confused child. "But you have been drinking. What's more likely, that old Jasper here has been a master card shark this whole time, or that you simply counted wrong?"

That seemed to placate Garret enough for him to sit down and pick his cards back up.

***

Now you might think that Zachariah diffused the situation there, but you'd have been wrong. All he did was light a longer fuse. The men kept throwing back drinks and playing like they were betting lives rather than a few dollars. Again, there was just an air that things weren't going to end well. More than a few of my regulars who weren't card players cleared out of the place, and I can't say I blamed them.

As the pot deepened and the evening turned into night, Eli's verbal sparring, once playful, had turned downright venomous. When Jasper put forth a bet that was a mite more conservative than others that'd been placed that night, Eli had some choice words for old Jasper. He put on a bad Irish accent and said, "Oh. Is that your whole bet? Sure you don't want to raise me a couple potatoes, or can you afford it?"

Now I swear to you that Jasper was the gentlest old man you ever saw. The closest thing anyone had ever seen to an act of malice from him was when he raised up a pickaxe to break some gold out of the earth, but he shot out of his seat like he'd been shot out of a cannon and lunged at poor Eli with his steak knife and slashed his old friend from ear to ear. Garret and Maxwell each grabbed an arm and dragged him back from the table, but they needn't have. The second he cut Eli, Jasper dropped the knife. It was like all the rage that had built up in him over the course of the night just, went away. I don't mean that as he let it out when he killed him. It was more like the anger that consumed him just disappeared like it weren't even his in the first place.

Before Jasper could quit stammering and say something, Zachariah scooped up his winnings and excused himself, saying that these boys weren't the type of folk he liked to keep company with, and just as quick as he'd come in, he was out the door.

"Y'all, what the Hell happened to us tonight?" Jasper asked himself just as much as he asked the rest of us. "The way we was acting tonight...that ain't us."

Garret was always the type to keep his cool, even in a tough spot. He was the first one to say what they were all thinking. "What made tonight different than any other? Zachariah. Who stood to gain from us going at one another like we did? Zachariah. Who walked away with our money?"

They all glanced at the door.

"I don't know how he did it, but he brought out the worst in all of us." Garret pulled his pistol from the holster on his hip. "I think we ought to give him a piece of our minds for what he did."

Having just watched Zachariah work his magic on these boys, I worried that maybe he'd talk his way out of it, but they were wise to it at that point. I saw the way that Garret held his pistol with his muscles loose so he could draw fast and the hammer already pulled back. There wasn't going to be much talking. I told them what he said to me about being dropped off by a wagon and that he had to be on foot. Clem even confirmed it, saying that she didn't see a horse tied off outside that could've belonged to him.

"Come on, y'all," Garret called out. "We can catch him before he gets to the stables, and he'll be easy to track in the snow."

I asked Clem to mind the bar and went with them. If I hadn't I wouldn't have believed what I saw. We stepped out into the snow and there wasn't a single set of footprints in the snow, only a set of what looked like the impossibly large hoofprints of some giant goat. I know what you're thinking. Hoofprints too big to be a goat. It's got to be a horse. I tell you here and now that they were goat hooves, longer and more pointed than the round prints left by horses. That's when we knew exactly who had been sitting at the bar with us, bringing out our worst inclinations for violence and hate. Garret tried to follow the prints, but they disappeared at the edge of town, and I've got to tell you, I'm glad they weren't able to track him down. A card game left one of our own dead. I can't imagine what would've happened had we confronted him. All I can say is that I hope he never darkens my door again, and I'll be wise to keep watch for a mysterious stranger descending on this place like some kind of plague.

I became inescapably aware of my mortality when Father passed away. Of course, the shadow of death already hung heavily over our family when my mother died giving birth to my younger sister, Lydia, but it always felt like an abstraction. Perhaps it was because I was so young that I could scarcely remember her face, or perhaps because

Mother's life ended as Lydia's began. Regardless of the reason, Father's passing made me realize that it was only a matter of time before death caught up with me.

My demise looming over me amidst the backdrop of corpses being returned from fighting for the Union on the docks of New London wore on me to the point where I felt I had to flee for the sake of my sanity. Since I had just recently returned from university, part of me thought that I should seek out a suitable wife and start a family, but ultimately I decided against it. If I were to start a family at that point in my life, it would have simply been to distract myself from death, and that felt worse than simply fleeing. Instead, I decided to strike out West, hoping that a year of adventure amongst prospectors and cowboys might distract me from the dread that had taken hold of my mind. Money wasn't a problem; it never was for the St. Germaine family. The only thing tethering me to life in Connecticut was my sister. Once I'd found her a suitable husband, I'd be free to try to outrun the inevitable.

It wasn't difficult to find suitors. Lydia was beautiful, well-educated, and quite charming, all characteristics that Father attributed to our mother's influence from beyond the grave. Of the several bachelors who wished to court Lydia, we both found ourselves charmed by a man named Samuel Winthrop, a physician from Boston, who had just recently set up a surgery in New London. I must admit that I was relieved that a man she found so intoxicating could also offer her the financial and familial stability that I wanted to ensure she had before I left.

After a short ceremony, I left the St. Germaine estate in their care and set out to the West. Most nights, the sense of novelty and adventure pushed the thought of death to a small corner in the back of my mind.

Then one night, I saw evil standing on two feet.

I had fallen into the routine of regular poker games with a few prospectors and drifters I had begun to think of as friends. I lost money to them every time, but I didn't mind. I considered it the price of admission to sit at their table for an evening of drinks and camaraderie. One night, a man in all black came in, and there was something about him that made us more boisterous, taunting, and reckless than usual. Before we realized we were under his influence, one of us lay murdered at the table, and the man left with his winnings, blood money. I wish I could say that his brand of evil was obvious, a direct attack on civility and goodness, but it wasn't. It was more insidious. He found cracks and insecurities in the hearts of good men and opened them until the hot blood of murderous rage flowed freely. Worst of all, we smiled and laughed as he did it.

I'd only seen that insidious charm once before. When I handed over my sister, my only living family member, and our very home to a man who plied us with expensive red wine, music, and a smile that one couldn't help but reflect back.

Of course, that recognition wasn't enough to get me to board a train back to Connecticut. At first, I thought writing a letter to my sister would be more prudent. But then I had the strangest dream. It was as if I were reliving the moments that led to Lydia marrying Samuel and me leaving for a life of adventure. But this time, I was an outside observer, and sitting in my place was the pale form of my father. He sat where I sat, drank the wine that I'd been given, and stood at the altar in the same position I had.

The only difference was his expression. Where I'd worn the smile I'd been trained to wear, his face was one of heartache. Each time Samuel filled Lydia's wine glass, his eyes widened with alarm, and when Father's ghost boarded the train to run away the same way I had, he'd given me a look of disappointment and frustration from my early adolescence when he expected me to behave like a man, but I wasn't ready.

He wasn't here anymore. I had to be ready.

That was when I knew I had to return back East. Writing a letter wouldn't be enough.

***

The train ride was long, and it gave me time to consider how unprepared I was. Truly, I didn't even know what I intended to do. Would I burst into our ancestral home and what? Accuse my brother-in-law of reminding me of a bad man I'd met while traveling. No. I knew something was amiss and that, in some small way, my father had reached out from beyond the veil to ensure I protected our family. I needed to discover the nature of Samuel's misdeeds before I could act on them.

I arrived at the family estate at dusk and simply watched it from afar for nearly an hour. The windows upstairs held no light, despite being among the first homes in the city to be set up for gaslight. The only glow came from the hearth in the parlor. I approached the door, and when I knocked, the door felt as cold as Father's old bones.

I heard some rustling, and then Samuel came to the door. "Maxwell! So good to see you." His smile held the same level of infectious charisma, save for the slightest moment's hesitation. "Did you write? We've received no word of your coming home to visit."

I knew that if I lied, he'd see right through it, especially if he was the master of deception that I thought he was, so I told the truth. "I just found myself struck by a sudden urge to see my sister. Is she here?" I glanced over his shoulder into the dark house that appeared to have fallen into disrepair in my absence. Lydia had always taken such pride in the house and seeing it in such a state only made me worry about her more.

Samuel glanced toward the stairwell and replied, "She's retired early for the evening. I'm afraid she won't be very good company tonight, but could we meet for breakfast?"

I didn't like the implication that I was expected to find lodgings when my family's home stood just before me, but I decided that being too confrontational could show my hand prematurely. I'd lost a lot of money playing poker out West, but at least I'd learned that lesson. "That sounds delightful. Is the breakfast at the inn still as good as before?"

"Even better, I'm told." Samuel beamed. "We'll see you there in the morning before I begin my work at the surgery."

***

My stay at the inn was less peaceful than I'd anticipated, but a small glass of the bourbon that I'd grown to like in my travels helped me fall asleep. I thought the dreams replaying memories with the specter of my father looking on with a disappointed grimace would have subsided after returning home. Instead, they worsened. My merciless mind transported me back to my first confrontation with death. After Mother passed, Father enlisted the aid of a wetnurse to care for Lydia, but he poured his attention into me. Perhaps it was his coping mechanism to keep himself too busy raising a son to mourn the woman he loved. In this dream, I revisited a night when I couldn't sleep.

The only difference between the dream and my memory is that our roles were reversed. My father sat on the floor crying for a mother's nurturing that would never come, and I looked down on him through my father's sad, tired eyes. I felt his desperation to let me sleep, to have a moment's relief from the grief that nothing could repair. His body moved on its own as I continued to watch through his eyes.

I Saw the Devil in the West

He warmed a cup of milk and then I felt him hesitate before he reached for a small glass bottle full of brown liquid. Father added some of it to the steaming cup before adding a dollop of honey, presumably to mask the flavor. When the small form of Father sipped the milk, my senses flooded with the memory. A harsh, bitter taste surrounded by the sweetness of honey and the comforting nourishment of warm milk. I remember complaining about the taste, and Father insisting that I finish the cup. A dull floating feeling came over me, and I remember that all the pain that kept me awake felt muted, as if I were submerged in a warm bath.

I caught the ghost of my father sitting in my place before he could sleepily fall to the ground, and I instinctively carried him to my childhood bedroom. His body hung limply until we walked past Lydia's door and he kicked open the door and we both saw baby Lydia being tended to by the wetnurse.

I awoke before dawn, covered in sweat, convinced that the persistence of my dreams was Father was trying to tell me what exactly was amiss from beyond the wall of death. I walked the waterfront, hoping the predawn stillness would help me decipher his message. The only epiphany I had was that Samuel very intentionally kept me out of the house. If I were nearby when he and Lydia left, I could have a few minutes to search for clues before they would arrive at the inn.

When they left, I found that my key still unlocked the house. I worried that Samuel would have changed the locks, particularly if he had something to hide, but he hadn't expected me to return. Once inside, I saw that the estate had fallen into disrepair, with cobwebs occupying the corners and a thin layer of dust on all but the most frequently used surfaces. I noticed that the general cleanliness of the house had been neglected, but there wasn't any real damage. Perhaps Samuel planned to sell the house. That helped me know to search for something that would not only endanger Lydia but also make her not care about the state of her ancestral home.

When I entered the kitchen, I felt cold, and despite the house being sealed, a cabinet door opened. I took it as a sign from my parents and opened what appeared to be a pantry for herbs and spices just above the house's stores of red wine, Lydia's favorite. Initially, nothing looked out of place. There was rosemary, thyme, and everything else a kitchen ought to have, but in the back, I saw a large brown bottle that brought me right back to the evening's dream. The label had been scratched away, save for a faded L-A-U. I opened it and the bitter aroma from my dream assailed my nostrils, confirming what I'd suspected. Father had given me mere drops to get me to sleep, but more had been snuck into Lydia's wine for some time. In my dream, Father was so careful with the dosage that I presumed that too much could lead to illness or death. That had to be Samuel's scheme. He had done well for himself as a physician, but being the sole inheritor of the St. Germaine estate would provide him with more wealth than he could have earned in a lifetime.

When I decided what I'd do to Samuel, the chilling breeze grew warmer and I felt Father's approval of the dark deed that brewed in my mind.

I arrived late to breakfast and begged forgiveness, saying that I lost track of time during an early morning walk. We exchanged pleasantries and I tried to keep the conversation going, despite the fact that Lydia seemed to be somewhere between drunk and asleep, an effect of the drug Samuel had been giving her. When Samuel asked how long I'd be in Connecticut and what my plans were, I changed the subject to tales of my travels in the West, all the while practicing the poker face that I'd learned among my friends at the saloon. Just once, I risked a question that might have made him suspicious. "Samuel. When I was in New Mexico I woke up with quite a headache, a hazard one faces after having developed a taste for whiskey. The physician gave me something for it, and I can't for the life of me recall what it was called. Was it lau–"

"Laudanum." He interrupted. "A common treatment for pain and insomnia. Why do you ask? Are you well?"

"I'm quite alright." I smiled. "I just want to know what to ask for next time."

"There's always a next time when it comes to whiskey. Isn't there?" He laughed at his own joke.

"When you've had genuine Kentucky bourbon, there's almost always a next time."

***

Samuel returned home after finishing his day's work, only to find Lydia and I sat at the head of the dining room table. "Maxwell…what are you doing in my house?"

"Apologies for arriving unannounced." I smiled and sipped from my glass of bourbon. "It used to be my house until I tried to outrun both the past and the future. That's the funny thing I found out. You can't. No matter where you go, the past is always with you, and the future is always waiting for you. Look at me, being philosophical when I should be welcoming you." I poured a glass of brown liquor to match the one I'd been sipping. "After our talk this morning, I thought it would only be right to share my last bottle of Kentucky bourbon with you."

Samuel accepted the glass and sipped. He coughed. "It's strong."

I took a long sip of mine. "I'd have offered some to Lydia, but she seems quite under the weather." I gestured to her, half asleep in the chair beside me. "Ironic that the doctor's wife is sick."

"Unfortunately, such things can happen." He began to sweat as he took another sip.

"Maybe give her some laudanum." I offered, revealing my hand. "Although I suspect you may be running low."

I Saw the Devil in the West

"What makes you say that?" Samuel loosened his cravat and started to look alarmed.

"I kept some," I explained, no longer caring if he saw through my facade. "Just enough to wean Lydia off it over a few weeks. That's what Dr. Chapman across town says is best. But the rest of it ended up in that bottle of bourbon…after I poured my glass of course." I raised a toast to Samuel.

Samuel stood to object to the accusation and caught himself shakily on the edge of the table. This time, I interrupted him. "You know, I saw the devil in the West. He reminded me so much of you, but you ain't him." I let a little of the accent I'd picked up in my travels come through. "You're worse. The devil can't help being deceitful. You're just a man, doing it by choice. A mortal man."

His arms gave out and he dropped, gouging his eye on the corner of the table as he fell. I finished the rest of my glass and watched him bleed. According to Dr. Chapman, someone who drank as much of it as he did wouldn't be waking up, and then Lydia would find herself a widow, with her estate restored.

I thought home was a place, but really it was a connection between the memories that make us up and the future we can't escape.

The ambulance roared down the winding backroad southwest of Boston as the snow started to fall. Norm knew he had to slow down. The ambulance had been stripped of most of its medical supplies, but the stash of illegal liquor from Canada weighed the vehicle down, and Norm knew he'd need to be cautious or risk sliding on the road.

"Come on, Norm." Edward jabbed at the driver. "We want to get out into the sticks before the sun comes up."

Thomas wanted to drive slowly through the towns to avoid getting noticed, but he knew that as the new guy in the crew, he should keep his opinions to himself. He'd only been with the gang in New York for a few months, and this would be his first run to Canada to bring liquor down into the city to supply the speakeasies that the bosses ran things from. He hadn't proven himself enough to have an opinion that mattered yet. All he knew was that the five years of prohibition had created opportunities for any man who was willing to take a risk. He also knew that he had two choices in life. He could go look for a job washing dishes or selling groceries, or he could take a chance and have a chance at being a big shot. It had been only a few months since he'd made his choice, and he thought he'd have doubts, but he didn't.

Norm downshifted and turned the car off the main drag and onto a road leading through southwestern Massachusetts. He figured a backroad through Massachusetts would lead to backroads through Connecticut, and then he could get on Route 1 into New York City and be home free. He'd made the trip dozens of times over the past few years and had been trying to perfect the route so he could tell the bosses about it, and then he'd be up for a promotion, maybe be the guy who organized the runs from Canada to New York instead of being the schmuck doing the driving.

An hour outside of Boston, the roads started getting slick. Norm slowed down to a crawl, despite Edward's complaints, and headed south on backroads.

"Hey," Norm called out. "I've got to take a piss. After that, how about one of you guys take the wheel?"

Edward climbed into the driver's seat and kept the speed down until he heard Norm start snoring. The ambulance kept accelerating as Edward thought about seeing his girl a night early. The more he thought about his girl, the less he thought about the road until a big deer darted into the road in front of him. He swerved to the right, and when he missed the animal, he swerved back, trying to correct the course of the vehicle and stay on the road, but that only made the heavy ambulance spin out.

When the three men stopped screaming, and the car slid to a halt just barely still on the road, Norm glared at Edward. "What in the Hell was that?"

"Don't look at me. It was that damned deer! It ran out right in front of us." Edward put his hands up defensively.

"I let you get behind the wheel for five minutes, and you nearly got us all killed." Norm scolded.

"Don't talk to me like I'm a kid, or I'll knock your God damned teeth in!" Edward shouted back, raising his fists.

"Alright, fellas. Might as well get out and check the damage." Thomas chimed in, hoping he could stop it from coming to blows between the two more experienced men in the group.

Norm sighed forcefully. "He's right. Beating the hell out of each other isn't going to get the booze to New York any quicker. If anything, we'll have to stop at a hospital, and they'll have all kinds of questions about a stolen ambulance. The best thing we can do at this point is to figure out if there's anything wrong with the car and get back on the road."

The Primeval: Meatwagon

The three men got out of the car, turning up their collars against the wind and standing in the beam of the headlights. Although none of them were mechanics, they looked at the engine, and everything seemed to be working, but when Norm put the ambulance in reverse and tried to back up onto the road, they heard a loud grinding noise.

Thomas saw an opportunity to prove himself and squatted down by the passenger side tire. "Put her in reverse again, Norm."

Norm put the vehicle in reverse and rolled ten feet back.

"I've got it figured out." Thomas declared.

"Well, spit it out," Edward ordered.

"The fender is rubbing against the tire," Thomas explained.

"Is that bad?" Norm asked. "Can we drive it like this?"

"It could be worse." Thomas stood up, trying to show confidence that he knew what the hell he was talking about. "We could drive a few miles if we keep it slow, but if it gets up to speed, the fender could cut the tire, and then we're in a world of hurt."

"Alright, boys. Here's what we've got to do. One of us has to take the ambulance into town and get her fixed up." Norm explained. "You guys are going to take the booze into the woods and hide out until I'm back."

"You're right. The idea of freezing my nuts off in the woods with Thomas isn't exactly what I had in mind, but it sounds a hell of a lot better than what you're talking about doing. Why are you so eager to be the one to go into town with the stolen meat wagon and take the risk?" Edward reasoned.

"Believe me. I don't want to be the one, especially since you were behind the wheel when this all happened, but I know it's got to be me. Thomas ain't much more than a kid, and I don't trust you to have the finesse to pull this off without getting us caught."

Edward wanted to punch Norm out for that last comment, but he knew that if the bosses heard that he was driving when things went bad, he'd be dead meat. "Fine, but we need to find a decent spot in these woods to wait for you. Even if we make a campfire, we need to find a spot that'll block the wind."

"Alright. It wouldn't hurt to know where to find you guys when I get back." Norm said.

Norm turned off the engine, and the three men trekked into the forest, searching for a suitable spot for Edward and Thomas to wait for Norm to return. Their top priority was getting far enough off the road that passersby wouldn't see their campfire from the street. Another mile into the thick forest and they came to a natural clearing that didn't look like it had been cleared by people, and in the center, a formation of rocks leaning into one another waited for them. At first, they thought that they could just use it to block the wind, but upon closer inspection, Thomas noticed an opening into the earth underneath the rocks.

The Primeval: Meatwagon

"I think there's a cave or something down here," Thomas exclaimed. "It'd keep up out of the wind and the snow."

"That sounds good." Edward chuckled. "You check it out."

Thomas looked at Norm to see if he'd stand up for him, but Norm's silence said it all, and Thomas knew he'd be the one going down into the cave to see if it was safe. Using alcohol meant to clean wounds and some bandages attached to a branch the size of a baseball bat, they fashioned a torch to light the way as Thomas explored the cavern.

"If I holler, you guys come in with guns drawn. Okay?" Thomas called out as he disappeared into the dark winding path into the earth.

"You've got a torch and a pistol, but yeah. You shout, and we'll come running." Edward laughed with peals of cruelty that let Thomas know that he was truly on his own.

After a few claustrophobic twists and turns so tight that Thomas started to feel relieved that at least there wouldn't be a bear hibernating in the cave, the narrow passageways opened into a large round chamber with a jagged stone formation in the center. He inched closer to the boulder in the center of the room and saw symbols on several of the jagged rocks that jutted out from the central mass. He only examined them for a moment and then got back to checking the cavern to see if they could use it. Thomas looked at the smoke rising off the torch and saw that a subtle draft above his head carried it down one of the passages and presumably out of the cave. When he was satisfied that making a campfire in the central chamber wouldn't fill the cave with smoke and kill them, he went back to the opening and got Norm and Edward.

"Yeah. This will do just fine." Norm exclaimed. "Hell. We might actually have to remember this as a decent place to stash the booze when there are too many cops on the roads."

"Sure...This could be a real home away from home." Edward sarcastically quipped.

Once they knew that they'd found a spot to hide out, they trekked back to the ambulance and got the suitcases full of liquor.

"Okay," Norm declared. "Get the goods back to the cave and sit tight. I should be back in a couple of days at the most."

"A couple of days?" Edward protested. Thomas felt the same way but knew that his protests would fall on deaf ears.

"It's the middle of the night. Even if I find an auto shop that's open, they won't start working on it until morning, and if they have to get an engine part from the next town over, that'll be more time. But trust me, one way or another; I'll be back in a couple of days."

"Alright. If we don't hear from you in three days, then we're going to assume you got pinched by the cops, and we're going to get the hell out of this place." Edward said.

"Fair enough," Norm replied with a long exhale. "I'll be back."

***

The Primeval: Meatwagon

By the time the sun began to creep over the horizon, Edward and Thomas had gathered enough dry firewood to create a bonfire in the main chamber of the cave. Since they didn't have anything better to do, they ended up making a few small fires around the cave so they could see more than just a few feet in front of their faces. Soon, the cave contained an orange glow that allowed them to keep warm and see their surroundings.

"What I wouldn't do for a steak right about now," Edward complained.

"I hear you." Thomas nodded. "As soon as we get back, I'm going to heat up a frying pan and make half a dozen pieces of bunny toast."

"Bunny toast?" Edward sat up straighter, suddenly more interested in what Thomas had to say.

"It's just a breakfast my old man used to make. You cut a hold in a slice of bread and fry an egg in it."

"Why is it called bunny toast?"

"No clue. That's just what the old man called it."

"Speaking of bunnies, maybe one of us could stay here and guard the stash while the other goes hunting. I wouldn't mind a little rabbit roasting over that fire." Edward suggested.

"You're a real city boy. Ain't you?" Thomas asked, letting a hint of his southern drawl creep into his speech.

"Grew up in Hell's Kitchen, and I hardly left since," Edward replied. "What makes you think that, though?"

"All we got are pistols." Thomas held up his revolver. "These things are useless when it comes to hunting."

***

Edward rolled up his jacket into a makeshift pillow and tried to get some sleep. He hoped that he'd wake up and Norm would be back with the ambulance running, and they could get back to the city. Thomas slowly paced around the cave, trying to concentrate on exploring his surroundings rather than think about the hunger that gnawed at his insides.

"Edward. Come see these symbols on the rocks." Thomas waved Edward over. "Do you think these were done by cavemen or something?"

Edward examined the symbols out of boredom more than genuine interest. "I don't think these are man-made."

Thomas perked up. "What makes you say that?"

"There are no signs of tools being used to make these shapes. It looks more like the rock just naturally wore away like that." Edward leaned in more closely.

"That's impossible." Thomas waved a hand dismissively.

"I know it's impossible, but there isn't a single sign that someone chiseled this into the stone. Feel it." Edward ran his finger down the length of one of the symbols. "Damn it!"

The Primeval: Meatwagon

"What's wrong?"

"You mean besides the fact that I'm squatting in a cave with you? I cut my damned finger on this stupid rock." Edward held up his finger, and blood trickled down the length of his finger and dripped into the symbol that had cut him in the first place.

"Here you go." Thomas rummaged through the small first-aid kit that he'd taken from the ambulance and tossed Edward a bandage.

Before Edward could bandage his finger, the world around them began to shake and rumble. The men made eye contact, and before they could even begin to think about what was happening, they both dashed toward the cave opening. Just as they got close enough to the opening that daylight poured into, one of the massive stones at the opening fell down, sealing them inside.

They pushed as hard as they could, but even with their combined strength, all they could do was push their own boots deeper into the mud just inside the cavern's narrow opening. Edward fashioned a primitive club out of a rock and a piece of firewood as thick as his arm, but in the cramped opening of the sealed cave, he didn't have the room to swing it with enough force to chip away at the slab of stone that sealed them underground.

"We can follow the smoke of the fires. It's got to be getting out of here somehow, and we can get out that way," Thomas suggested.

They followed the path of the smoke, moving as quickly as they could without risking the possibility of missing any vital details that could save their lives. The paths twisted and circled back, making the two men wonder if there were deeper depths of the cave than they'd originally thought. After what felt like an eternity of searching, they found a narrow passageway that went upward at a steep incline.

"Looks like a tight squeeze," Edward declared. "You'd better be the one to go."

"I won't be able to hold a torch in a tight space like that without burning my face off, and your fat ass won't fit up there." Thomas handed his torch to Edward and began worming his way up the claustrophobic cavern using his sense of touch rather than sight.

Thomas snaked his way through passages so narrow that the stones scraped his stomach, and he'd begun to believe that if he couldn't find a way out, he'd be trapped there forever. Just as he was about to give up hope, he saw light coming from somewhere above him. With hope in his heart for the first time since the cave-in, he started squirming toward the light, and soon he tasted cool fresh air that made him realize how stale the underground air he'd been breathing was.

His hope left as quickly as it had come when he wormed his way forward only to find the passageway too narrow for anything more than his arm to reach through. At best, he could raise a hand to the surface but nothing more.

The Primeval: Meatwagon

By some miracle, he was able to worm his way back down the tunnel and into the larger cave. He reported what he'd seen to Edward.

"Any way you can widen the opening so you can get out?" he asked.

"I wouldn't be able to pull the stones out of the way. It's too narrow for my arm to move much," Thomas replied.

"Maybe if you climb up, pistol first, you could shoot it into the air to signal where we are," Edward suggested.

"I thought about that too, but if someone came running, they'd find two New Yorkers with pistols and a case of illegal booze down here. We'd go from being locked up down here, to being locked in a cell. The only person we want coming for us is Norm, and he already knows that we're down here. I say we sit tight, and when he sees that we got caved in, he'll figure out a way to move that big rock."

"Either that, or he'll just leave us for dead down here," Edward uttered cynically.

"He won't do that." Thomas gestured to the cave's main chamber, where they'd stashed the liquor. "If he gets back to the boss empty-handed, it'll be his head. He knows where we are, and he knows what we've got. He'll be back."

***

What felt like days later, Edward woke up Thomas, shaking his shoulder violently. "I heard something in one of the passages. Hooves or something."

Thomas rubbed the sleep from his eyes. "What? That's impossible. We checked to see if there were any animals in here before we decided to hide out down here."

Cloven-hoofed footsteps echoed through the cavern, and the orange glow of the fire seemed to get brighter. Edward's eyes darted around the chamber but saw nothing. The hooves clicked across the stone floor again.

"Did you hear that?"

"Yeah," Thomas replied. "But it's impossible. God, I wish there was some sort of an animal down here."

Edward looked at Thomas, aghast at his wish. "Why on Earth would you want there to be something down here with us?"

"We checked around here pretty good, but you know how these tunnels twist around like a maze. If there's something down here, maybe it got in through another passage that we missed. Either that, or it's been trapped in the cave with us the whole time. If we follow it, it could lead us to a way out, or if it's stuck down here too, we can shoot it and roast it over the fire so we at least have something to eat.

More footsteps bounced off the chamber walls, followed by a shadow of antlers on the cave wall opposing the large stone in the center of the chamber. Edward saw Thomas's eyes widen at what he saw, and the shadow seemed to glide across the rough stone wall as Edward turned around with a torch in hand.

Edward passed the torch from his right to his left hand and pulled the pistol from where he'd tucked it into the waist of his pants. He stood in a low stance and stealthily crept towards the passage where the shadow seemed to be coming from. He glanced down the narrow passageway and then turned back to Thomas.

"Get your gun and go around the other way."

The two men wandered in the dark, darting in and out of the labyrinthian passageways, waving torches and casting shadows. Thomas heard echoes of the hooves on the stone floors but also the heavy footfalls of Edward's boots. He looked away from his torch and tried to focus on the darkness so his eyes could adjust. The hooves got louder and louder until he couldn't tell what direction they were coming from until he turned a corner and bumped into a stone wall.

When he fell, the torch landed in his lap. He cried out and quickly grabbed the handle of the torch and tossed it to his side. The flame grew and grew as if it had rolled into a bottle of kerosene, making the entire area glow. The only thing disrupting the orange glow on the stone walls was the shadow of a long face with huge antlers that could never have fit in such narrow passageways. Thomas raised his pistol and fired three times.

Edward screamed and fell to the floor, clutching his shoulder. His howls of pain reverberated off the labyrinthian cave walls, making a sound like the suffering of dozens of men. When Edward's howls evolved into words, Thomas rushed to him and held the torch to examine the wound. The bullet had gone into his left shoulder and hadn't gone through the other side, which Thomas knew meant something but didn't remember if it was good or bad. When he saw the way that Edward's arm hung limply, he reasoned that the bullet had hit a bone in the shoulder, stopping it from coming out the other side and made the limb useless.

Thomas reached out to place a hand on Edward's shoulder but thought better of it before making contact. "Oh shit! I'm sorry, Ed. I thought you were...I don't know what I thought you were."

"It's just us down here, you fucking maniac!" Edward shoved Thomas away with his good arm.

"Just let me help you bandage it."

"Get away from me!" Edward shouted, the roughness in his voice due to anger as much as pain. "You've done enough."

Thomas stepped forward and reached out. "Really, Ed. You'll need a hand if you want to wrap that up."

"I said, get the fuck away from me!" He shoved Thomas again, harder this time.

With the second shove, Thomas tripped over his own feet and fell backward, hitting the back of his head on the unforgiving stone of the cavern's walls. Stars hung in his vision, and something in him, ancient as a stone dagger, woke up, and he charged at Edward, tackling him to the floor. Edward lashed out with the ferocity of a wounded animal and slammed his fist into Thomas's ribs. Every movement he made caused pain to shoot down the length of his arm, but it only made his rage hungrier for violence. He punched Thomas's face until the sounds of impact sounded wet, and it reminded him of his uncle Andrew packing meat at his butcher shop when Edward was a kid.

As the beating continued, Thomas knew that Edward wasn't going to stop until he was dead. He reached for the torch, and as soon as he felt it firmly in his grip, he thrust it into Edward's face, blinding him in one eye and briefly setting his dark hair on fire.

Edward howled once more in pain, in rage, in hunger, and he lunged forward, biting a chunk of flesh out of Thomas's neck. As the blood trickled down his throat, he felt the kind of power that only made a man want it even more. An insatiable lust for violence consumed him as he tore into Thomas in the dying light of the ancient cave.

***

Norm parked the freshly repaired ambulance right where it had crashed only days earlier and hiked into the woods, the fresh New England snow crunching beneath his leather boots. He almost didn't recognize the stone pillars that made up the entrance to the cave now that they'd been knocked over, but when he examined it more closely, he saw what had happened. Norm tried to pull up the stone by hand but quickly realized that if he kept it up, he'd throw out his back, and then he wouldn't be a help to anybody.

He went back to the ambulance, and between the vehicle's jack, a few branches, and some tools that he'd scrounged from the back of the cab, he'd rigged a system that allowed him to lift the heavy stone and push it aside enough for him to get down there.

Norm smelled death when he got down a few paces, and he wondered if one or more of the others had gotten themselves killed in the cave-in. He considered the possibility that they'd died and decided that either way, the suitcases of liquor would still be there, and he could still get them back to New York in time. As he crept around the curved path, he heard the crackling of fire and, after a few more paces, saw the slightest hint of its glow.

"Ed! Tom! You alright down here?" When he heard no response, instinct guided Norm's hand to the pistol holstered on his hip. He drew it and held it in front of him as he stealthily worked his way forward.

He saw Thomas's body first. Strapped to a thick branch and propped over a large fire, how could he not? Then, just as Norm's mind began to reel with what could lead a man to commit such an atrocity, Edward stood up. Norm almost didn't see him at first. His shirtless body was caked in so much blood and dirt that he blended in with the earthen wall of the cave. Norm looked at the man and saw the eyes of a predator.

The Primeval: Meatwagon

Both men stood still, eyes locked on one another for only a few seconds that felt to Norm like ages, and then Edward charged at him.

Norm raised his pistol and fired four of the six shots into Edward's chest. The bloodied man fell back against the giant stone pillar in the center of the cave's chamber, leaving a streak of blood on it as he fell. Norm saw the beast of a man's chest rise and fall weakly, but he didn't want to leave anything to chance. He stood over Edward and fired the fifth shot through his skull.

His eyes darted around the cave chamber, partly looking for the liquor but also searching for any movement. He sensed nothing, but he did see the handle of one of the suitcases by the warm glow of the fire. Norm briefly considered making two trips into the cave so he could still hold the pistol in one hand as he got the liquor up to the surface, but every fiber of his being told him to get out of the cave as quickly as possible. He holstered the pistol, picked up the two suitcases, and scrambled out of there as quickly as he could.

He pushed the stone over the cave opening as best he could, sealing the horrors that he'd seen away, and he made his way out of the forest and into the ambulance.

As the ambulance roared away from the Massachusetts forest, Norm thought about what he'd tell the boss when he got back to New York. He decided that he'd tell him that Edward had turned out to be a snitch and that Thomas had gotten killed in the crossfire. He'd say that he took care of the threat to his boss's operation and buried them in a forest, but he made a promise to himself that he'd never tell anyone where they'd actually gotten stuck. He'd never do anything to run the risk of returning to the hellish place he'd barely escaped.

He threw out the map and bought another one at a gas station, where he chose another route for next time, one that steered clear of this forest.

Shana followed Maggie on her bicycle down one of the half dozen dead-end roads that made up the Oak Circle Estates community. The name seemed oddly out of place given the fact that the circle at the center of the housing development only contained a tiny oak tree, recently planted where the ancient oak once stood before it had been torn from the earth and burned away. The town considered renaming the neighborhood after everything that had happened but decided against it because it would just be another in a series of disturbing headlines about what had happened in the development of homes that were becoming increasingly hard to sell with each news cycle. The difficulties selling the houses had unexpected benefits for people with good timing though. Neither Shana nor Maggie's families could have afforded the houses they'd bought in that neighborhood before the three reductions in price. Shana's family moved from a double-wide trailer across town, and every morning that she woke up in a bedroom of her own rather than one shared with her seventeen-year old older sister made her glad about the change of scenery. Maggie's family moved from Texas after her police officer father investigated a missing person's case that took a toll on him, but after a few weeks of forcing herself to talk like the other girls at school, only a select few knew where she'd come from. Among them was Shana, who had quickly become her new best friend after moving in next door to her.

"Did you know that back when they were building these houses, a giant oak tree used to take up almost all of that circle?" Shana nodded to the skinny oak tree that had replaced its ancient ancestor five years earlier.

Maggie squinted, trying to imagine what it looked like before. "That explains why they named it Oak Circle Estates, but then why did they take it down?"

The Primeval: New Beginnings

Shana's eyes darted back and forth across the neighborhood, confirming that nobody was within earshot of her and Maggie. "Are you telling me that nobody told you about what happened?"

"Shana. You know that you're the only one who tells me anything about Hopeville. Hell, most folks around here don't even know where I'm really from." Maggie let a hint of her accent show, reminding her friend that only a few months earlier, she'd been living in Amarillo, Texas.

"I guess it's not the kind of thing the adults in town tell people when they decide to move here. It's the sort of thing that they pretend to forget... that way, maybe the rest of the world will too."

Maggie tilted her head, signaling a growing impatience. "Come on, Shana. Out with it already. I thought people up here were supposed to talk faster than the rest of us."

Shana's expression grew more serious. "Okay, but promise not to tell anyone about it." She didn't wait for a response. "Back when they were building this place, some weird stuff happened. First, they thought one of the construction workers went berserk and killed a bunch of the other workers one night."

"Bullshit." Maggie drew out the word to make it sound like more than just two syllables.

"I swear to God." Shana raised her right hand. "And it gets weirder. Turns out that it wasn't that one guy. It was actually a group.

Some kind of freaky cult. They were taking people into those woods and killing them, and eating them. The only reason people found out about it was that a few of the construction workers that survived the first night found out about it."

"No way! I know I was just a kid living in Texas when it happened, but it would have been all over the news," Maggie protested.

"I'm serious. The mayor kept it all quiet because the leader of that group of people was some kind of big deal in the city hall," Shana explained.

Maggie hesitated. She wanted to believe her friend but was afraid that she was falling for some sort of trick. Perhaps an initiation prank for new kids in the neighborhood. She considered the possibility and decided that it was unlikely that Shana was trying to trick her. There was no audience, and Shana seemed more serious than Maggie had ever seen her. "So the other construction workers, the ones who survived. They found out about it, and then what? They called the police?"

"They didn't want to call the police with no proof. They figured everybody would say they were all PTSD after what they went through, so they tried to find proof, and the people in that cult caught them."

"Did they get away?" Maggie had fully bought into the story.

"Barely. One of them died, and the other two were all battered up," Shana said.

"And what about the cult dudes?" Maggie asked. "Are they still around?"

"Some of them died in the chaos. That's how the tree got chopped down. I guess they worshipped some monster that they said lived in the tree or something, and they chopped the tree down and set it on fire as a distraction so they could get away."

Maggie hesitated. "You said that some of them died in the chaos. What about the rest of them?"

"The police got a bunch of them. Some of them were still in the forest, and they rounded up the rest through phone records and stuff." Shana spoke in hushed tones. "When the police rounded them up, they all said that it wasn't them. They said that a monster lived in the woods and that it was the one doing all the killing."

Maggie said nothing. She just stared at Shana and waited for her to explain more.

"There's no monster out here, obviously. The woods aren't big enough for some Sasquatch-type thing to be roaming around without someone getting a video of it. The police checked the forest, though. They found bodies, but no monster. After everything was said and done, they took those psychos and locked them up in Hopeville Valley Hospital in the insane asylum part of it."

Maggie shivered. "Do you think any of them got away?"

Shana shrugged. "Who knows? They wouldn't be able to stay here though. The police would have all their information from the others. If any of them got away, they're probably living in another country by now."

"I bet they all got caught." Maggie sighed. "If they're that kind of crazy, they'd probably slip up and get caught by the police somewhere else."

A mischievous smile stretched across Shana's face. "If you're so sure about that, then why don't you spend the night out here?"

Maggie fired back a knowing glance. "Do I look that stupid to you? You expect me to camp out here all alone, freezing my ass off, just for you to sneak up in the middle of the night and scare me?"

Shana replied, "Honestly, that didn't occur to me. Now that you mention it, it seems like a good idea though. How about this? We stay out here one night together, and then anyone who wants to hang out with us has to do the same thing…" Her grin grew wider. "And that's when we sneak out at night and scare them."

Maggie replied, "Okay. Do you have a plan?"

"After dinner, get some camping stuff and put it in your backpack. Make sure you're wearing all black before you leave. I'll tell my parents I'm sleeping over at your house. You tell your mom and dad the same. Then meet me by the Oak Circle Estates sign at eight-thirty. That'll give us enough time to find a good spot to camp out for the night."

The Primeval: New Beginnings

***

The girls met at the wooden sign that read Oak Circle Estates in large golden letters, Shana on foot, Maggie on her bicycle.

Shana looked Maggie up and down. "What are you doing?"

"What?"

"You brought your bike?" Shana chortled. "We're going into the woods. What good is a bike going to do out there?"

Maggie looked down at her bike. "I guess I'll lock it to a tree or something."

After twenty paces of dragging her bicycle through the vegetation, Maggie found a tree skinny enough to get her bike's lock around, but sturdy enough to actually anchor the bike to that spot if someone did find it and try to take it. She locked her bike to the tree and followed Shana deeper into the woods. The foliage was much thicker than it was back home and in some ways reminded her of what a jungle might look like. Maggie looked down as she walked and followed Shana's wagging ponytail as if it were a compass, navigating her journey into the unknown.

A short while later, Shana stopped. "It looks like there used to be a dirt road here, but it's all grown over." She turned and followed the remnant of a path.

Suddenly, Shana froze, forcing Maggie to walk into her. Maggie wanted to ask why Shana stopped, but when she looked up, she didn't need to. The girls stared at the ruins of an old cabin. The wood had begun to rot and the stairs leading to the front porch had disintegrated, but the windows had remained intact and the roof seemed to be stable.

Shana hesitated, suddenly just as mystified by the deepening lore of the forest as Maggie. "What do we do?"

"You mean to tell me that you didn't know this was out here?" Maggie said without taking her eyes off the corpse of a home.

Shana gulped. "They said that one of the construction workers built a cabin and never left the forest after that first night because his brother died, but I would have thought they'd have either torn it down or sold it to somebody, not just left it like this."

"...Do we go inside?" Maggie asked her normally confident friend, almost afraid to hear her answer."

"I think we have to," Shana explained. "If we don't check it out, we'll just think about it constantly, wondering what might be inside. I'd rather see it for myself than lay awake at night imagining what might be in that house."

***

Maggie took the opportunity to look brave in front of the usually much more confident Shana and turned on her flashlight before using it to gesture for her friend to follow her. The two crept forward onto the rotted wooden front porch, testing each step before putting their full weight on it. Maggie held up the flashlight high over her head and shined the beam on the doorknob. They stepped inside and saw an open main room with a wood-burning stove that looked like it hadn't been touched in years. There was a record player on an end table next to a dirty old couch, and a circular kitchen table resting on an angle after something had chewed through one of its legs.

When Shana turned on the flashlight function of her cell phone, Maggie whispered, "Why do you have your phone on?"

"Because I wasn't born in the nineteen eighties." Shana gave her friend a sarcastic smirk. "Wait. Why are you asking me that?"

"My mom has some app where it tells her the GPS location of my phone. If she looks at it and sees that I'm in the middle of the woods, she and my dad will be out here, and that'll be worse than a monster or some cult of creeps."

"Oh. I don't think my mom has that," Shana squeaked as she turned off her phone. "Do you have another flashlight?"

Maggie reached into her backpack and pulled out an LED flashlight small enough to fit in the palm of her hand. She decided to keep the long metal flashlight with four batteries in the handle for herself. Its beam of light wasn't as bright, but the fact that it could also function as a metal club made her feel safer. They explored a room right next to the front door, which turned out to be a simple bathroom with nothing there to frighten them other than a few dying spiders between the window panes.

They continued to explore the two remaining rooms in the tiny cabin, beginning with a bedroom that held a bookcase and a queen-sized mattress that took up nearly the entire room. The books on the bookshelf were mostly biographies of musicians that neither of the girls had ever heard of and books about people traveling the world. Shana remarked that it was a strange choice for someone who had apparently become something of a hermit in these woods during the last months of his life. The final room appeared to be a study containing a desk, a chair, and a corkboard with pieces of paper pinned to it. The papers, yellowed by years of sunlight pouring in through the window contained furiously scrawled notes that they could barely read and most notably, a charcoal drawing of a large humanoid creature with long fingers and antlers like a deer protruding from its head and mingling with the branches of the trees that had been penciled into the background.

Shana reached out to touch the drawing, but hesitated mere inches away, as if making contact with it would awaken something that slept in the forest. "Do you think that's what those people believed was in the woods? It looks like he believed in it too."

Maggie lowered the flashlight from the drawing. "This guy lost his brother the first time those people came after him and his friends. To him, they were the monster."

Shana stepped back. "Maybe we should get out of here. In fact, maybe we should just get out of the woods and go back home."

The Primeval: New Beginnings

Maggie placed a reassuring hand on Shana's back. "We can get out of this cabin, but we have to stick it out for the night. If either of us goes home, then our parents will know that we snuck out."

The girls quietly left the cabin, careful not to touch anything and they continued into the forest until they found a small clearing where the ground wasn't covered in rocks and roots. Maggie, the more experienced camper, in the group pulled a sleeping bag from her backpack and rolled it out on a soft piece of earth. Shana did the same.

The two girls lay on their stomachs next to one another looking out into the darkness, and talking about the local legend that Shana had passed on to her friend. They debated the possibility that there actually was a monster in the woods at some point. They agreed that it couldn't live there during modern times, but Shana theorized that perhaps something lived in the woods in times of antiquity, serving as the basis of the fantasy that sick minds constructed and that others had latched onto over the years. Soon, the silence of the forest overtook their conversation and they stood gazing into the darkness, punctuated by the lights of fireflies on the midsummer night. They fell asleep on the soft earth to the sound of branches blowing in the gentle summer breeze.

Hours later, Maggie woke up to the sight of a deer walking in front of them, a mere fifteen paces away. It stopped between the two girls and stared in their direction, its pointy antlers reaching out toward them. At first, Maggie's mind tricked her into thinking that she'd seen the monster, but before she could scream, she saw that the creature that stood before them was just an innocent inhabitant of the woods, a victim more than a monster. Animals like this one were hunted for sport and run down by cars every day. After hearing tales of the monsters that had done horrible things in these very woods, Maggie decided that this deer was not among them.

Maggie realized that there really was a monster in these woods all those years ago, but it wasn't a monster that lived in the trees. It was a monster that lived in sick hearts and broken minds. Thinking about the darkness that could dwell in regular humans made Maggie feel nervous and she began biting her nails, a bad habit that she'd developed in sixth-grade algebra class when the lessons got boring and she needed something to do with her hands. She winced as she accidentally bit a piece of her cuticle, drawing a tiny drop of blood. Maggie instinctively put her hurt finger in her mouth and sucked on it. She tasted the coppery taste of blood, and she thought about the human monsters who preyed on their own kind in that very forest and she realized that the malevolent spirit of the forest had left along with them. The self-destruction and violence had faded away and all that lived in the forest that night was companionship and the gentle harmony of creatures like the deer that she watched disappear into the fading darkness.

Death arrived first, parking her motorcycle, a black 1940 Harley Davidson Knucklehead in the back row of the parking lot of the diner closest to the side of one of the roads that served as the main connection between parts of the country before highways overtook them with their sheer efficiency in the 1950s. Still, she preferred the backroads for the personality they injected into her eons-long existence.

She sat in the diner waiting for the others as if she was always there. She preceded everyone else and was always the last to leave a room. The waitress seated her, introduced herself as Shelley, and filled Death's coffee before heading back behind the counter. Her coffee was as black as her clothing and steam rose off it mirroring the ghostly shade of silvery white that she always colored her hair, regardless of if she came in the form of a twenty-year-old or an old woman. Lately, she'd been favoring the form of what humans called "middle-aged" conventionally attractive enough that the humans looked at her either out of admiration, lust, or jealousy, but with enough signs of age to serve as a constant reminder that death…she was inevitable.

Her black leather boots tapped on the linoleum floor as a reminder of the asbestos buried beneath layers of modern upgrades, but not gone, never gone. Just like her.

Shelley stood by the coffee pot and checked in on the few regulars who preferred sitting at the counter, mostly older men who had been sitting in those same seats nearly every weekend since she took the job, pregnant, eighteen years earlier. She looked at the sameness of it all and wondered how fine the line was between stability and a dead end. Still, she couldn't complain. She managed to give her daughter, Katherine a decent life and sent her off to UConn. She could never have done that bartending, and moving to a new apartment every six months like she'd been doing before Katherine came into her life.

"Did she order anything?" Robbie, the cook asked as he peered between the opening in the wall that separated the kitchen from the rest of the diner and nodded his head in the direction of Death's table.

Shelly didn't react at first, caught up in looking out the door and at the road where everyone seemed to be going somewhere. Everyone but her. "What? Oh. No. She's waiting for a few more people."

Four Horsemen Meet in a Diner

"Are you alright?" Robbie ignored the eggs frying and looked at her thoughtfully. "You seem a thousand miles away."

Shelly put her customer service facade back up and smiled. "A thousand miles away? Maybe someday, but now we've got a breakfast rush to survive."

Then came War, riding his Harley Davidson WLA, still painted green from its original use in World War II. He couldn't help but park at an angle, that occupied two parking spaces. His favorite thing about humanity's tendency to carve up and lay claim to the land was that it created the concept of occupied territory. When he entered the diner, he kicked the dirt off his boots on the border where the cracked pavement of the parking lot and the doorway of the diner met. He pulled the baseball cap off his short-cropped hair and made eye contact with Death before joining her at the booth. War made sure to pull up on the waistband of his pants to make the forty-five caliber pistol holstered on the right side of his hip visible for a fleeting moment to only the most vigilant people dining.

"I see you're early, as always." War sat on the edge of the booth with one foot claiming ground in the aisle.

Death smirked. "I suppose you could say I've always been here."

"Suppose you're right." War turned his attention to the waitress, whose curly brown hair draped over the shoulders of the uniform dress the diner required and probably had for a long time. "Excuse me, Miss. Could I trouble you for a minute?"

Shelly put on a smile that had come with years of practice. "It's no trouble. What can I do for you?"

"My…" War's voice trailed off. He'd almost said sister but realized that he looked like an eighteen-year-old man. "My aunt and I are expecting a few more relatives. Could you switch us over to that booth over there?" He gestured to a corner booth that could easily fit six, but in a pinch could comfortably seat eight. The diner had just opened and soon that booth would be needed by a larger party, but War couldn't help but sneak small conquests into his day.

Shelly looked at the booth and then back at War. "I don't see why not. Go on and have a seat there and I'll be right back with new place settings. Would you like a refill on that coffee ma'am?"

"Always." Death slid the coffee mug to the edge of the table and Shelly topped her off.

***

They moved to the corner booth, War's latest conquest. He stretched out and admired the extra space he'd claimed. Death found his little victory amusing but didn't want to encourage him. War had always done a good enough job of patting himself on the back. Instead, she removed one of her black leather gloves and caressed the petals of a potted flower sitting in the window so she could watch it slowly wither.

Four Horsemen Meet in a Diner

Just something to pass the time while the waitress came back and set down paper placemats with advertisements for local businesses ranging from real estate agents to dog walkers. "Can I get you something besides coffee, or do you want to wait until the rest of your party arrives?"

Before Death could finish her sip of coffee, War cut in. "Yeah. I'll have the steak and eggs, and a big pile of home fries. I'll have the meat bloody, the eggs over medium, and the home fries crispy. You got that?"

Shelly gestured with her pen to show she'd written down his order. "Got it." Then she eyed Death. "How about you, ma'am?"

She considered waiting but thought better of it when she remembered Pestilence's table manners. "I'll have the spinach omelet."

"I'll get those started for you. Just let me know if you need anything." Shelly walked away and checked on the few other tables that had people at them. They were in Gina's section, but Shelly took care of them. Gina was late to work, probably having a hard time dropping her kid off at daycare again. Shelly didn't mind. She'd been there back when her girl was little, and besides, Gina always made it right when they split up the tips at the end of the shift.

***

Famine parked his Honda Grom sport bike next to Death's and thought about how he could have tainted the soil at the little farm up the road to make it so nothing would grow there for years. Ultimately, he decided to leave it be. There would be more opportunities soon enough.

He opened the door and looked across the diner for his brethren. Famine made note of the dozen booths and another six stools at the counter slowly filling up with people as the morning wore on. He wore a thermal henley shirt the color of a dead wheat field with the sleeves rolled up above the elbow, and even with the added padding, Famine barely filled out the black T-shirt that hung off his gaunt shoulders. To look at him, one couldn't rightly tell how old he was. Either a middle-aged man that puberty never quite hit or a young man who had been through Hell. He saw Death and War occupying the corner booth and walked over to join them.

"You're looking well," Death said as he sat down, and you could see every vertebra bump up beneath his shirt to show that Famine was little more than a skeleton with skin and hair.

"Good to see you." War tipped the brim of his baseball cap down. "Looks like the last horse just crossed the finish line." He eyed the door.

Pestilence shoved the door open, conjuring a cacophony from the little bell attached to the entryway, and loudly coughing into her right palm before closing the door with the same hand. The way she kept her sunglasses on indoors and ran her fingertips across every booth as she walked by might have made the casual observer think she might be blind, but the horsemen who knew Pestilence knew she wore the sunglasses to hide the bloodshot eyes, nearly crusted shut with infection, and the constant touching of everything was to leave little remnants of disease on surfaces that others might touch and so receive her sacrament. She stopped by the table. "I'm just gonna swing by the bathroom before I come to sit with you." Pestilence coughed loudly.

"Take your time," Death stated coldly. Even though none of them could die and everything, even bacteria, died the second it touched her, Death always found Pestilence's presence distasteful. Of course, nobody knew death better than Death and she considered herself the ultimate connoisseur of it. The way Pestilence left people dying in piles of their own shit, vomit, and saliva teeming with microscopic life eating them from the inside out lacked something essential. It didn't have the elegant complete feeling of someone dying of old age surrounded by the people who love them, or the purity of someone cut down by gunfire dying for a cause they believe in with every ounce of who they are, whether that cause is personal, or ideological. It didn't even have the quiet desperation of one of Famine's deaths, which was an acquired taste Death had learned to appreciate. To use the language of humans, Death considered War and Famine family, but Pestilence would forever be a colleague.

Pestilence returned and sat down at the edge of the booth, opposite War. "You should see the microbes in the bathroom here. Over 74,000 different strains of bacteria in one room!"

Before anyone could reply, Shelly returned to the table. "Welcome. The other orders are almost up. What can I get you two?" She held up her notepad toward Famine and Pestilence.

"I'll have the omelet with spinach, mushrooms, and peppers." Famine ordered and then eyed his compatriots knowingly.

Pestilence sneezed and ordered. "Some bacon, rare. Nice and chewy. Follow that up with the runniest sunny-side-up eggs you've ever seen on top of some toast." She waited for Shelly to finish writing down her order and then continued. "However runny you're thinking, go a little runnier than that."

"I'll be sure to tell the cook." Shelly tried not to look visibly disgusted, but she knew she was a much better waitress than she was an actress. "Anything to drink?"

"I'll take a black tea with cream," Famine said.

"Just a mug of hot water. I bring my own tea bags," Pestilence announced with an air of superiority.

"I'll get your orders up. I'll just be a minute." Shelly checked on the other tables on the way to the kitchen. Gina had arrived and rushed to wipe a stain off her blue dress before going out and taking a few of the tables off Shelly's hands.

***

"You're looking healthy, well I guess I mean you're looking well," War said to Pestilence.

"Oh, things have been great these past few years." Pestilence sniffled. "Things used to ebb and flow. Some decades I'd be starving, others I'd be flush, but I worked out a way to stay well-fed all the time. Believe it or not, War, I've got you to thank for that."

"What'd I do?" War leaned back in the booth and reached out with both arms, his fingertips encroaching on the space of the booth adjacent to theirs.

"Those stunts you pulled with the Great War and World War II. Bloody brilliant!" Pestilence exclaimed. "You went so big and it must have been so good, but you almost took it too far and wiped out the humans. At first, I was pissed off at you. I thought we were going to have to wait for some other species to evolve to a point where we could have our fun with them, maybe even on another planet depending on how many nukes the humans could manage to launch before they wiped each other out, but no. You pulled away at the last minute. Made it last." She sat lower, melting into her seat, imagining what War felt when he pushed the world to the brink and stopped at the last minute. "It's really what you've done since then that gave me the idea. Sure there haven't been continent-spanning, potentially world-ending wars lately, but you've kept yourself fed with little wars and conquests on all sorts of scales. You've always got something going. You're never craving, but never satisfied…you're always being satisfied, which is the best."

"I suppose when you put it like that, things have been pretty good." War laced his fingers behind his head. "I get all the satisfaction without that pesky post-extinction clarity. So how'd you manage it?"

John Opalenik

Pestilence smiled from the corner of her mouth. "All it took was a few rumors, a mean Tweet here or there, and I convinced enough people that it's their God-given right to get sick so that the rest of the population will just have to live with it." Her smile faded as she thought of a moment when she could have been defeated, at least temporarily. "With medicine getting better and all those vaccines, I thought I might have to live a small life until one of you all cut the humans down to size again, but as I said, a few whispers in the right ears and I convinced them that medicine would hurt their kids and that avoiding the plague…well, like the plague would be some form of cowardice that would steal their freedom or whatever. It's actually amazing how little I had to do. Just a few little pushes and the humans took care of the rest."

"Some of them." Death cut in. She couldn't let Pestilence be too pleased with herself.

"Enough though." She leaned forward and coughed. "There may be folks who know how to keep me at bay, but they send their kids to the same school as them that pray at my altar. They go to the same concerts, football games, and grocery stores. I don't need them all to worship me. Just enough to force the rest into putting up with me forever."

Famine looked like he was going to say something, but stopped when Shelly returned and put their food on the table. She looked at him with sympathetic eyes. "I'm so sorry, but all the peppers seemed to have gone bad. It's the strangest thing. We can substitute something in like

116

maybe tomatoes, or we could just put in a new order. What would you like to do?"

"Tomatoes would be great. Thanks," Famine replied smiling.

When she left, Famine continued. "Y'know…I did something similar, but I wasn't thinking about either of you when I thought it up."

Death looked around at the diner and the customers eating, in some cases, more calories in a single meal than other people would consume in a week. "In some places, sure. But when I look around here, the only one who looks like they're starving is you."

He leaned forward to get a packet of sugar for his tea and when his abdomen should have touched the edge of the table, Death saw his ribs poking out from beneath the canopy of his shirt. "Oh, Death. You're just not looking closely enough." Famine turned and gestured to the teenage daughter in a family of four sipping a soda to go with her breakfast. "Diet Coke. She can drink and drink and not get a single calorie of sustenance from it. And look at that guy." He nodded toward a heavyset plaid-clad trucker shoveling down an egg and cheese sandwich as he kept one eye on the window where his truck waited to continue its journey.

"He seems satisfied." Death smirked.

"No. Look past him and see that big truck in the parking lot he drove in on. There are whole towns of people who wouldn't have a single scrap of food if guys like him stopped making deliveries for just a week." Famine closed his eyes and shifted his weight in his seat to hide his

117

arousal. "So many people just a few bad turns away from starvation, and they're fine with it. Oh, I may not look it, but I'm so well-fed."

"Careful there, Famine. You'll lift the table up with all that excitement." War chuckled at his own joke.

"You give him too much credit," Death countered.

***

"He wants tomatoes instead of the peppers." Shelly stepped back into the kitchen to avoid anyone flagging her down to their table for a minute.

Robbie turned to where they kept the produce. "You've got to be kidding me."

"What?"

"The tomatoes went bad too!" Robbie raised his hands in frustration when he thought about how many orders he'd have to change before the morning ended. "Maybe something happened with the refrigeration last night. Did the power go out or something?"

"I don't think so, and if it did, wouldn't everything else have gone bad too?" Shelly thought of what could have happened. "Maybe it's that thing that happens with apples."

"What are you talking about?" Robbie asked.

"That old saying that one bad apple can spoil the bunch. It's actually true." She always had a knack for remembering seemingly useless fun facts. "One of my biology professors mentioned it in a lecture back when I was in school. When an apple gets rotten it releases ethylene which makes the rest of them start to rot too. Does that happen with peppers and tomatoes?"

"I don't know. I didn't even know about ethylene until you told me about it." Robbie returned to the griddle and then turned back. "Y'know Shelly, you should go back and finish that degree one of these days."

She smiled. "Sure, Robbie. Just as soon as Katherine finishes hers."

***

Shelly returned looking genuinely disappointed. "You're not gonna believe this, but the tomatoes went the same way as the peppers."

"How about onions instead?" Famine offered, just a little too pleased with himself.

"Got it. Be right back." Shelly rushed back to the kitchen.

Death watched her go and then gave more thought to her younger siblings' talk of how they can keep pushing things to the brink and then teeter back and forth on the edge of oblivion. Flirting with that one big rush that would be impossible to match for millennia but never going all the way. She realized that she'd taken for granted the simple fact that she was inevitable, and they were not. Sure. Humans found ways to live a lot longer than they used to in ages past, but all that could ever buy them was a few decades, which were like grains of sand on a beach to her. Death thought about bragging to her siblings about the fact that she'd never have to worry about a lapse in gratification, but she decided to keep it to herself. They'd use that as a bargaining chip when it came to paying the bill later.

Shelly came back with Famine's omelet. "Sorry about all the trouble. Who needs more coffee?"

Death held out her mug and War pushed his to the edge of the table for her. Pestilence loudly reminded the waitress that she brought her own tea bags and that yes, she wanted more hot water. Shelly took care of the coffee right away and brought out the hot water before taking a cigarette break. She didn't smoke but decided she'd get cigarette breaks just the same, just to relax rather than get a nicotine fix. Instead of freezing her ass off out back, she lingered in the back of the kitchen near Robbie, the short-order cook, and vented, sometimes about the job, sometimes about everything else. He was a good listener and she had a feeling that he was into her. She could see herself feeling the same way. She liked his tattoos and the way his hair looked halfway put together but suggested that he put no effort into styling it. He looked like the sort of guy she'd woken up next to and never seen again too many times when she was young, but the way his hair had gone salt and pepper, and his tattoos faded made him feel safer, like a guy she might wake up next to and would actually stick around for breakfast. She thought about it, but from her days bartending, she knew that making something of their mutual attraction was a bad idea as long as they worked together.

Four Horsemen Meet in a Diner

"Did you see that table out there? The goth cougar, the army kid, the tall skinny guy, and the anti-vax mom." She let out an exasperated sigh. "They look like some sort of fucked up family reunion."

"The one with the food we kept having to send back?" Robbie asked as he flipped the pancakes for table two.

Shelly looked down at her fingertips. If she had a cigarette, she'd have taken a long drag. "Yeah, and you'd have thought the Karen who can't stop coughing, would've had the pain in the ass order. I mean, yeah. She can't shut up about bringing her own teabags like ours aren't the same store-brand bullshit she's got in her purse, but at least she didn't send anything back."

"It's always the quiet ones, I guess..." Robbie's voice trailed off and he looked away from the griddle to make thoughtful eye contact with Shelly. He saw something in her eyes that she wasn't saying. She was choosing to vent about the little things instead of what was really on her mind. "You doing okay though, Shelly?" He didn't want to pry, but over the years he'd learned that Shelly was the kind of girl who kept too much inside. "You've been quiet since your daughter went off to college."

Shelly blinked back a tear. She didn't want to get serious during her fake smoke break, but there she was. "It's just a lot of little things. Sure, it's expensive but I don't mind. I've been broke before, but this time it's so she can go to school and not have to bartend after class like I did–" She knew if she kept going she was going to cry and spend the rest of her shift all puffy eyed with people wondering what just happened. "Can we talk about it later?"

Robbie simultaneously felt bad for asking and even worse about upsetting her on what should have been a break, but it also seemed like she needed to let it out. "Sure. Buy you a drink after work?"

Shelly knew how that would end despite both of their best efforts, and that didn't bother her, as much as the weeks of awkwardness wondering if it was the alcohol or if there was really something there. She decided to keep it simple. Just some time spent with someone who cared. "Dinner. My house."

He smiled with a warmth and familiarity that told her that he understood all the subtext of that slight change of plans and was okay with it. "Yeah. That sounds really nice."

***

Famine proudly chewed the omelet that was crunchier than it ought to have been. "The onions went bad too. They just sprinkled in onion powder and hoped I wouldn't notice."

"But you did." Death's voice was flat. She didn't bother hiding the fact that Famine's little games bored her.

"I did, and I love it."

Death gulped her coffee and briefly wondered how many cups she'd had since sitting down. War gnawed on one of the last bits of steak on his plate. Pestilence walked across the diner to go through the sugar packets on each of the vacant tables, making sure to touch them as much as she could. Eventually, Gina stepped away from her tables to check on her.

"Do you need something, ma'am?"

Pestilence wiped her nose. "Do you have any stevia packets?"

Gina glanced at the identical trays of sugar packets. "Just sugar and Sweet and Low."

"I need something all-natural to put in my tea."

"Isn't sugar all natural, from the sugar cane plant?" Gina usually knew better than to argue with a customer, but she was so sick of people coming into a middle-of-nowhere diner and expecting it to be something it was not.

"Poison ivy is a plant too. Do you want me to put that in my tea?" Pestilence made a show of gagging at the thought.

Gina bit her tongue and thought of something to offer that might actually shut her up. "We have honey. That's a safe, all-natural way to sweeten your tea."

"I know they say it's safe, but think about it." Pestilence tapped a mucus-coated fingertip to her temple. "They say it's not safe for pregnant women or babies, but then they just expect the rest of us to suck it down without even questioning it. I'm not saying it's poison or anything, just suspicious."

Just as Gina's composure was beginning to crack, Pestilence looked down and announced that she found a loose stevia packet in her purse and walked away immensely pleased with herself.

She returned to the table where War rested a palm on his gut. "What happened to you?"

"Little wars break out all the time, whether they're little conquests like small city drug dealers arguing over territory or a nation annexing a region of their neighbor's land. They happen every day and I feel all of them."

"And you were worried about me getting too excited," Famine quipped.

"Right. You all seem like you've had enough." Death slid her empty mug to the center of the table. "Now who is going to pick up the check this time?"

"War seems like he's fine," Famine asserted. "Isn't it my turn?"

"You know we don't take it in turns," Death countered. "We never have."

"I might as well get it," Pestilence offered. "I already left little surprises all over this place for anyone who left early to bring home."

"That doesn't mean anything," War argued. "Let me have this one. It's been a while since I got one."

"Right. Because what's going to happen? Is some army going to parachute in and occupy the diner? Come on," Pestilence countered.

Four Horsemen Meet in a Diner

"You know it doesn't have to be like that," War growled.

Death's patience waned. "You three just spent our entire breakfast bragging about how good you've got it lately. I think it's only fair that I get mine this time."

"The only reason you didn't join in is that you've always been well-fed," Famine argued. "All you have to do is wait, and you get what's yours."

"Just like crops die even without your help, conflicts happen regardless of War's influence, and people will get sick whether or not Pestilence is there to encourage it." Death leaned forward and exhaled a cold breath that made the other three shudder at the thought of what it would be like to be mortal. "I'm taking this one, and you three can fight it out next time."

The others eyed one another and then nodded in agreement. War spoke for them. "We'll wait out front."

***

Shelly took a step to where the kitchen met the counter and looked out at the tables filled with the same linoleum, the same food, the same experience playing out over and over again. Sure, the sameness was something that some people liked, in fact, a lot of her regulars ordered the same thing and even sat at the same booth every week. But it wasn't what she wanted. It never was. She pulled Gina aside.

"Shelly, is everything alright? That table of weirdos is gone. I picked up their check for you, so if they were bothering you half as much as they were bothering–"

"It's not that," Shelly whispered. "Listen, Gina. I need a favor."

Gina couldn't tell if it was something serious or if Shelly just needed Gina to cover her if she left an hour early, maybe to go to the bank and put her tips in the bank before they closed so she wouldn't get an overdraft fee when her bill's autopay feature drained her bank account. When Shelly looked at Robbie, as he flipped his fiftieth over-easy egg of the day, and then glanced back at Gina, her smile gave Gina all the subtext she needed. She'd been hoping those two would get together for years. They'd both spent their twenties dying to live and then the next twenty living out the consequences of all those nights out and mistakes that at the time felt so good to make, and they both came out the other side bruised, but better than they were before. They deserved a win. They deserved each other. "I've got you. It's been slow anyway." That last part was a lie and they both knew it, but it left them both with an understanding.

Shelly approached Robbie and asked him to come out to her car. At first, he thought she had a flat tire or a dead battery and needed a jump, but after a few not-so-subtle hints, he put two and two together and they went out through the door in the back of the kitchen to the back parking lot and Shelly's van.

Four Horsemen Meet in a Diner

Death came out of the bathroom, having killed the tens of thousands of microscopic bacteria just by being there, and eyed the patrons of the restaurant. The trucker was just finishing up his syrup-soaked pancakes. His truck along with its flammable cargo was parked close enough to the building to be part of what she had planned. The table of four was in their own world, the parents in a bubble of conversation about something of no consequence while the teenagers sitting across from them were lost in the limitless void of their phones. The two twenty-somethings still sat standoffishly across from one another, on a first date that would have been an only date regardless of Death's interference. The second waitress darted across the space, too busy to notice much outside of her typical duties. Death noticed that their waitress wasn't there and neither was the short-order cook, but that would work to her advantage.

She used the chaos of a college football team coming in all at once on their way from their university to that of their would-be opponents to climb over the counter and slip into the kitchen where she confirmed that the cook had left the space vacant. She looked around at all of the implements of death the kitchen had to offer. There were countless knives, and a vat of hot cooking oil, but that seemed too messy. She always found fire to be so much more elegant. Instead, Death opened the valves on all of the stovetops, fryers, and used a small knife to cut any hose that she could find leading from the five-foot-tall propane tanks on

127

the side of the restaurant. While the gas started to flow into the kitchen with a hiss that would have alarmed anyone but her, she thought about how long she'd have before people noticed the smell and what they might do to stop her. Next, she found the stairs heading down to the basement and turned the valve to cut off all the water coming into the building, including the sprinkler system. Death thought about the days when wooden buildings were heated with wood stoves and didn't have sprinkler systems. It was all so much simpler back then.

Next, she took one of the long matches meant for starting the grill they kept out back and made a makeshift torch out of a dishrag, a long metal spatula, and lots of cooking oil. She nearly threw the bottle back into the kitchen but instead sprayed the remainder of the cooking oil on the ground around her so anyone who might try to stop her would have unstable and flammable ground to contend with. Death returned to the space behind the counter, climbed on top of it as if it were an ancient altar to her, held up the flame, and waited for the gas to fill the room.

"Look! That crazy bitch climbed up on the counter with some sort of torch," one of the football players shouted.

"A little early to be drinking, even for me," another called out as he held up his phone.

The commotion caused the elder sister in the family of four to glance up from her phone long enough to film the scene playing out in front of her as best she could with her hands shaking, first from laughter, and then with fear when she smelled the gas. Having been lost down internet rabbit holes many times, she'd seen videos online of what a little propane tank attached to a grill could do. She didn't want to imagine what one made for an entire restaurant was capable of. "She turned on the gas! We've got to put out the fire." She shouted to anyone in the diner willing to hear, although she didn't get up to do anything. She simply kept filming.

The trucker heard her, let the syrupy bite of pancake drop from his lips, and glanced out the window toward his truck. He saw the white bubble of the propane tank half eclipsing his view of his truck, which was his only way out of the blast zone.

Some rushed her, others pushed for the door. Gina tried to guide anyone who would listen to the back door. Everyone who rushed the door got so close that the person at the front of the crowd couldn't pull the door open. He shouted for them to step back but only the first few people behind him heard, and when they pushed backward, the rest of the masses shoved forward, easily overpowering them. None of them were willing to take one step closer to the fire and the acrid smell filling up the room.

Standing confidently atop the counter, Death basked in the sheer power of what was happening around her. A few of her congregants tried to get the makeshift torch out of her hands, others were simply trying to hurt her. If anyone got close to making contact, she batted them away with the torch. There were those who tried to put out the fire by throwing

129

glasses of water at her which she dodged effortlessly, and anyone who would have tried to tackle her off the counter had to work their way through the crowd, many of whom were struggling to stay on their feet on the oiled floor. It slowed any of their momentum to a crawl. The others were pleading, asking why, begging. Amidst all their efforts, Death remained keenly aware of the fact that any time she wanted to she could throw the torch back into the kitchen and the whole diner would erupt. Still, she preferred to draw out the moment and savor it. Sitting atop a linoleum counter fashioned into an altar, it wasn't the first time Death felt that there was a fine line between begging and prayer.

Death waved the torch more intentionally now, setting alight anything that she could reach that would accept the flame, from dish rags to napkins. The cooking oil she'd sprayed ignited, and suddenly those who were trying to stop her began writhing in burning agony and tried to extinguish their burning clothes. They saw running away as a last desperate act of self-preservation, but Death knew that she'd simply turned them into mobile torches.

***

When Shelley got Robbie back to her van, he stopped kissing her long enough to hesitate. "Are you sure about this? We've known each other a long time and–"

"That's what makes me sure." She tried not to get sentimental to the point that their pent-up passion cooled down. "We've waited long enough. I don't want to wake up one day and realize I never took the one chance that mattered." She grabbed him by the shirt and pulled him into the back of her van.

Both Shelly and Robbie thought about how they'd both wanted this for a long time, and wondered why it hadn't happened sooner. When they started working together, they were both seeing someone else and despite the fact that they'd nursed one another through each of those breakups, nothing happened. If it had, it would have been a rebound that had more to do with their exes than with each other. In a strange way, Shelly was grateful for the time they'd hesitated to make a move. It made both of them certain that being together had nothing to do with anyone but each other.

She sat him down in the back seat and he squirmed his black work pants and boxer shorts down to his ankles, and then when he realized how ridiculous he'd look to her with a white T-shirt on top and nothing on the bottom he pulled the shirt over his scruffy hair. By the time he could see her again, she'd unbuttoned the front of her dress and hiked up the skirt to attempt to turn it into the sexy Halloween costume version of the waitress's uniform at the diner and climbed on top of him. Her last thought before instinct took over was that the reason she hadn't made a move earlier was that if things didn't work out, she'd be risking a precious friendship and that she'd finally taken the risk that would forever change the familiar routine she'd fallen into over the past several years. Lost in their own world that included only the back seat of the van and one another, they didn't notice the smoke beginning to rise from the building they'd just left.

***

A whooshing noise like a grill the size of a panel van being started escaped their notice, but the combined boom of the brick building, the glass shattering and screams being swallowed up by the fire all at once cracked the air in a way that nobody within a mile of the diner could ignore, let alone Shelly and Robbie who were still in the back of Shelly's van at the far end of the parking lot. Shelly looked over Robbie's shoulder, out the back window of her van, and saw the tail end of the explosion when the sound made her flinch noticeably enough to break Robbie's focus on her, he turned with her and they looked through the hatchback window of her minivan that cracked in the shape of a spiderweb when a piece of debris hit it. At first, Robbie wasn't sure what he was seeing and started to return his gaze to Shelley.

"Holy shit, the diner!" she shouted as she turned Robbie's head away from her breasts and toward the destruction over her shoulder.

Robbie saw the ball of fire expand and engulf the truck which then created its own explosion. He didn't know what the truck was carrying, but clearly, it was flammable. "Get down!" he shouted as he pushed Shelly off him and down onto the floor of the backseat of her minivan. He grabbed the fleece blanket that had been at his back the whole time they were together that Shelly had put there to keep her black dog's hair off her beige upholstery and he pulled it over them as he fell on top of her in the back of the van. Despite the thick blanket over them, Robbie felt the tiny particles of glass hit him like hail and could have sworn he felt the warmth of the fire. He held Shelly tightly and waited for the oblivion of an explosion to wash over them, but when it never did, he slowly peeked out from beneath the blanket. When he saw that whatever happened was over, he pulled the blanket off Shelly. She buttoned up the front of her dress and climbed back onto the seat, careful to avoid debris that could cut her knees as she looked back at what used to be the diner.

Normally, they wouldn't be able to see the front parking lot from the far end of the back parking lot, but the fact that the diner had been flattened by the explosion with the exception of the linoleum counter made it so they could see all the way to the street where four motorcycles waited, occupied by three of the four people at her table. Among the blasted-apart building and burned bodies, one figure remained intact, that of Death slowly rising from her linoleum altar with the ineffable satisfaction of a sufficiently fed and worshiped deity. The orange flames that rose from the torn-apart fabric and body parts turned black as she walked past and formed a gown of destruction and death that clung to her as walked and then fell to the ground, extinguished after she passed by.

Shelly and Robbie stared wide-eyed through the blasted-out hatchback rear window at the impossibility of anyone walking away from that blast, let alone so calmly. Robbie reached for the door handle, but Shelly grabbed his wrist and stared into his eyes with an intensity that told him the situation. They were in the presence of a predator and anything could provoke a deadly reaction.

Death walked to her brethren and started the engine of the motorcycle. She revved the engine and the four sped down the backroads of a world that they'd continue to feed on until no one remained to pay the tithe.

Acknowledgements

This collection would have been possible without the support of my amazing wife, Amanda, who not only provided the art for the book, but is a strong supporter of us keeping a household where reading, writing, and art thrive. Whether it's a book, piece of art, or a kid, I love everything we create together.

I'd like to acknowledge and thank my friends and colleagues in the horror writing community I've met through the HWA. There are far too many to name, so I'll stick with a few from the local chapter. The moral, and sometimes technical support of friends like Bert Piedmont, Jackson Kuhl, Logan Johnson, and BC Bull.

Thank you to everyone at Stokercon 2025 who encouraged me to push to release this collection.

John Opalenik